LIFE ST⊙RY THE
— OF AN —
ISLAND
GIRL

by

Ann Labbé

Grosvenor House
Publishing Limited

This book is published by
Grosvenor House Publishing Ltd
28-30 High Street, Guildford, Surrey, GU1 3EL.
www.grosvenorhousepublishing.co.uk

A CIP record for this book
is available from the British Library

ISBN 978-1-78623-732-3

PART ONE

Chapter 1

The garden was large; untamed, the trees, close together, spread their branches and converted the place into a tropical green chaos. Two huge bougainvilleas, one orange, the other pink, shared the old wall and covered its dark surface of volcanic stone with their dazzling colours. Nearby, an old rose bush showed off its voluptuous red blossoms. Lilac trees hid the entrance gate, giving a mysterious but romantic appearance to the property; their persistent perfume was overwhelming. A few mango trees, looking puny with their skinny, narrow branches, seemed to be waiting for the summer to delight every one of us with their sweet and mellow fruits. When I was a little girl, I knew every corner of this garden by heart; I loved it every day of my life. I used to pick up the camellias that had fallen from the shrubs to let them float in the fresh water of the fountain. I spent hours watching the tiny red spider or the green lizard, which lived hidden in the trunks of the banana trees. The garden was my refuge; I stayed there, avoiding the adults who had the bad habit of giving me insipid orders. My dreadful aunts could not stop exerting their power over me, the youngest girl.

The white house with yellow shutters, surrounded by a thick hedge of bamboos, belonged to my grandma. She lived there with her dearest daughter, Clothilde, the eldest of her children, who wore her widowhood like a humiliation. This aunt had very fair skin, nearly translucent. She avoided the sun by every means, and never went out for a walk. Her face was quite ugly, with red fleshy lips and protruding glassy eyes. The woman never stopped lamenting herself. All day long I would hear her say to my grandma:

"If my poor John were still alive, this would never have happened. Nobody would have dared do such a thing if he were here." Once a teacher, after her retirement she had nothing else to do but watch the garden and all those living there. I was her pet hate, and she was always spying on me behind her lace curtains. Sometimes she asked me about my parents' private matters; I replied vaguely but politely that I did not know anything. Then she complained about my lack of respect towards her. I listened to her, shy and unable to answer back, because I was taught not to contradict an adult. But deep in my heart I was filled with rebellious thoughts.

The members of my family were not overwhelmingly affectionate to me, so I spent much of my free time confined to the garden, feeling comfort and joy, listening to the chirping birds. I liked to observe the black ants, the ones that did not sting; they were my friends, so laborious, never lonely, working in harmony. I watched them admiringly. Those little bugs knew how to function, follow a trail, stop to whisper something in their comrades' ears and then go on fulfilling their duties with such acceptance. I spent hours simply sitting in the garden, observing its most silent and smallest occupants. I usually sat under the longan tree, a reading book on my knees. My dog, Tex, would lie close to me. I cherished these moments of peace. My solitude in this garden was very precious. I am thankful now that my parents did not notice me, giving me the pleasure of being on my own. They were unaware that their indifference would form me into someone independent, capable of finding happiness without the help of anybody else.

My parents, my brother and I lived in the second house, right in the middle of the garden. There was a third house facing the next street belonging to my mother's other sister. Our house was unfavourably located between the two others, so my family and I could not leave the premises without being seen by either of my mother's sisters. But Clothilde was the dreaded one. She was like a mischievous cat, sharp at noticing anything that moved. She never listened to the radio, and the slightest noise in her surroundings would prick up her ears. She was always on alert, waiting for the postman as if he were the Messiah, rushing to collect the letters first. She inspected the letters addressed to my parents suspiciously and opened any that attracted her attention. Then she licked the envelope with her thick tongue to glue it again, and gave me the letter saying:

"Bring that to your place, I do not want your father to think that I open his mail."

But if there was a letter for me from any of my pen friends, she kept it and gave it to my father when he returned from work. She wanted him to know that boys wrote to me.

Sometimes we caught her bent under one of our windows, eavesdropping; the summit of her black head appearing just above the sill. We hushed immediately, pointing a finger towards the intruder. My parents never accused my aunt of spying on them. There was a silent pact preventing my parents from confronting the rest of the family. Any conflict had to be avoided, out of respect for my grandmother. Aunt Clothilde was her protégée, so she had more rights than anybody else.

When I was a little child, I was totally insignificant in Aunt Clothilde's eyes. She was not even aware of my presence. But as I reached adolescence, she suddenly started to look at me. What she saw obviously displeased her. She would have done anything to stop me from growing up. She used to stare at me with her globular eyes, screening me from head to toe, and I would instinctively bend my back, hiding my growing breasts. She liked to ask my mother the most indiscreet questions about me. Their continuous whispering behind my back gave me the worst feelings of shame. I thought something impure was happening within my body.

On Christmas day my brother and I would go to my grandmother's place to wish her and my aunt a Merry Christmas. Grandma was welcoming on that day. She was not at all a cuddling person, but I was quite content with any sign of her affection; maybe a small pat on the shoulder after the usual peck on the cheek. But then I would have to kiss Aunt Clothilde's powdered cheeks. She perfumed herself with 'Paris' from Yves Saint Laurent, and she always put a mint sweet in her mouth to conceal her bad breath. This combination of scents defined her, and I held my breath when I got close to her face. Year after year the scenario would repeat: I would kiss her, trying to touch her cheek as slightly as possible while murmuring 'Merry Christmas' furtively. She totally ignored me, her eyes fixed on my brother. With her ridiculous, rough voice, she would say to him:

"Louis! Merry Christmas, my good boy! Here's your Christmas gift from your Aunt Clothilde, who loves you so much."

She would hold out some rupees to him. Then. turning her fishy eyes to me, she smiled mischievously:

"Maybe next time I'll give you something too, if you're nice."

Humiliated, but smiling as if I did not care, I would go home without telling anybody what had happened. I understood the silent messages my relatives sent to each other. My aunt waited for Christmas to let me know how much she disliked me. The worst part of it was that I was forced, each year, to go to her for the greetings. I could see how she enjoyed this moment, the only one when she had the opportunity to take revenge on me.

My aunt's nastiness started after she lost her husband, John. Before that, she seemed happy, but until that time

I was not aware of her as a person; she was just part of my environment. John was a captain and in charge of the island harbour. He died suddenly from a heart attack, leaving behind him a desperate wife and a no-less-desperate mother-in-law. But they were crying for themselves. With John dead, both women thought they had lost their supremacy over the other members of the family.

When my uncle John died, I was in a deep sorrow. Uncle John was big and looked great in his white captain's uniform. He had beautiful honey-coloured eyes that sometimes reflected sadness, as if he were aware of his approaching death. This man was the most gentle and caring person in the family. He was so lovely and so kind, especially towards us children. My brother and I adored him; he was the everyday Santa Claus, calling us with his loud voice before he drove off in his huge Vauxhall. We never missed any of his invitations for a drive, and we rushed happily to get into his car. It was usually just to go five hundred metres down the road, to the next shop owned by a Chinese man who seemed to love my uncle as much as we did. We always left the shop with our pockets full of multi-coloured sweets. On Sundays we went to the harbour with our uncle, and I remember how tiny my hand felt in his as we proudly walked along the quay. Sometimes he allowed us to visit one of those huge cruise ships, full of friendly white people with wrinkled faces. There was always a noisy bustle before the departure, and then the ship would leave the harbour slowly while the passengers waved at us. Back at home, a kaleidoscope of images would whirl through my mind for the rest of the day. What a happy time.

For the Christian celebrations, John bought an enormous knuckle of Serrano ham and tons of other delicacies, which were carefully put in the huge Frigidaire. We stood around him like flies, and gave him a hand unpacking everything. The next day, the whole family would gather together for lunch, al fresco, in the shade of a flowering vine. The men and women drank an aperitif while savouring the delicious amuse-gueule. Then my father announced proudly that the main dishes, cooked by him of course, were to be served: roast venison and a coq au vin. For hors-d'oeuvres, there were prawns in home-made aioli with a fabulous salad of palm hearts. Different wines were served generously to every grownup. My cousin Josephine was in charge of the desserts; she baked one of her delicious genoise cakes, and her lemon sorbet was served between the main dishes. The day went on with laughter and music in the air. The Chivas Regal and the wine getting heavier in their heads, the men discussed politics passionately; while the women gossiped about everybody they knew, forgetting to scold us children for making too much noise and running around restlessly with our new toys. Our gardener and Therese, our nanny, naturally took part in the festivities, but my aunts' domestics never joined them. Therese drank her whisky some distance away, sitting under the longan tree and snapping her tongue in appreciation. I liked to join her when I was tired; she gave me a warm toothless smile and we sat watching the others while the enormous sun went down, setting the sky on fire. All of a sudden a black veil fell on the houses, giving the signal to everybody to return to their own houses, satiated, drunk and happy.

Chapter 2

I was eleven and it was school holidays. I was in the third house, spending the afternoon at Aunt Juliet's, laughing at Josephine's silly jokes. All of a sudden, we heard my grandma calling for help. I remember seeing her; she was a small, fragile figure in black from head to toe, with her hair severely tied together in a knot, and she stood at the front door waving her arms desperately. We all rushed to her place to find Uncle John lying in his bed with half-opened eyes. A thin trace of white foam was coming out of the corner of his mouth and his finger-nails had a strange bluish colour. I knew he was dead. Aunt Juliet, quite naturally, started to pray the Paternoster in my uncle's ears, while Josephine called for a doctor. She had given me her baby to hold, and I was swaying it to and fro mechanically. Aunt Clothilde, reacting quite stupidly, I thought, was putting socks on her dead husband's feet. When the doctor came, he could do nothing but confirm the death of her husband, and she fell to her knees, horrified.

The death of my dear uncle turned the life of everybody living in the garden upside down. Sadness overcame the place. My grandma and her daughter Clothilde spent the rest of their lives moaning, their minds riveted to the past, revolted by the fact that it was John who died and not somebody else in the family, preferably my father. The wheel of fortune had turned; from that time, jealousy took over. The two women hated my father even more because he was in good health and enjoyed life. I must say that he was quite arrogant and had an attitude that others disliked. He had a good income as an engineer, was an attractive man, had a strong personality and worst of all, he was from a higher social class. Aunt Juliet hated him as well because her husband, Marcel, was quite the opposite: he came from a modest family, and he was a dusty notary clerk with a grey aura; a bigot who spent his free time at church and played the violin at weddings. He prayed kneeling on his prie-dieu in his bedroom and of course, this gave reason to my father to make fun of him.

When my father bought a brand new car, Aunt Clothilde bought a new one three days later, the same model. Marcel brought it back from the dealer because Aunt Clothilde did not know how to drive a car. But she had to buy a new car; she had to show to the neighbourhood that even if she had lost her husband, she was still as rich as before. Buying that car caused her some trouble because it attracted a lot of dubious men who phoned her night and day, asking for money. Soon enough, Aunt Clothilde's life became very boring. She had nothing to do at all, because my grandma took care of all domestic matters. Clothilde's main occupation now was to live a life full of jealousy and resentment. She wanted to know everything about each of us, even our deepest thoughts. She was afraid that we might be happier than she was, and this thought was unbearable. She did not want to hear us laughing or singing; we should not show any sign of happiness at all. That was why she started to manipulate. She found out everybody's little secrets and cruelly divulged them openly. She became the expert in malicious gossip. She did it in a refined way, never raising her voice or showing any sign of nervousness or aggressiveness. She was displeased to see my physical transformation, changing into a tall and slim young girl who attracted people's eyes.

My mother used to buy me clothes from France or Italy, and I wore them with pleasure, even if they were imposed on me. She insisted that I had very bad taste, and I was not given the liberty to choose anything. But people complimented me for what I was wearing, and I started to discover my own femininity. The thin little tomboy with short hair and scratched knees, who loved to climb trees and ride her bike, had metamorphosed into a gracious young girl. My mother was the fashion expert of the family, so she also bought clothes for her sister, Clothilde, who never left her home except to go to the bank or to church. I soon found out that my mother bought the same clothes for her sister and for me. I was an adolescent and really appalled to see that my aunt, a woman in her forties, was wearing the same shirts or sweaters as me. The woman boasted about how we were both wearing the same size, hiding her round belly under a stiff corset. I was angry with my mother, who did not even bother to listen to me, but put on this strange, half-hidden smile. But whenever she could, she told everybody how naughty I was, how ungrateful. I was sure that she was taking pleasure in seeing me suffer. My mother could be cruel. She was envious because I was daddy's girl; my father got on well with me, spent time talking to me, even discussed politics with me. We would argue sometimes, but he had some respect for me and we were on the same wavelength most of the time. My mother was always complaining about how her husband did not show any interest in her any more. There was a problem between them that was beyond my understanding. But whatever it was, I paid for it until her death. My mother's strange behaviour accentuated the whole uneasiness between Aunt Clothilde and me.

Aunt Clothilde was quite a poor soul, leading a life with strange rules. She retired early, but she stayed the teacher she had been, always immersed in the same book of French grammar and proverbs, *Le Bescherelle*. She never learned how to cook, never even boiled an egg. My grandma cooked for them both. When she died, my mother brought Aunt Clothilde's evening meals to her. Soon enough, they started to quarrel because my aunt constantly criticised the food. Exasperated, my mum asked her sister Juliet to take on the task.

Aunt Clothilde was a diva and was always prepared to show off in front of the few people she knew. She met some women at church during Sunday mass; there were two twin sisters, old spinsters who always put too much powder on their faces, probably to look whiter than they were. These women liked to compliment my aunt for her outfit and this brought her much pleasure for the whole Sunday. For some time she put her whole interest in a young girl coming to church with her mother.

She seemed to be obsessed by that girl. My aging aunt gave her sisters a full account of what the young one had been wearing on that particular Sunday, how it seemed that her buttocks were getting bigger, and how even the priest had a look at them during communion!

My aunt's aim was to look rich in front of all these people. She spent days in her bedroom, choosing an outfit for the coming Sunday or for Friday mass. She opened her huge ebony wardrobe and meditated for hours, contemplating her treasures. Finally she took out an outfit and hung it near the window in full day-light. The next day another suit or dress was laid on her bed. By Thursday she had made up her mind, and then it was time to choose accessories. She owned an immense number of shoes and bags, not to forget her jewellery, which she kept in a safe. She was always over-dressed, but she never reached the class and elegance of my mother, and was, without doubt, the ugliest member of the family. As time passed, she developed an alarming resemblance to a bull terrier.

Influenced by my old nanny, Therese, I was convinced that my aunt had the evil eye. When I was nineteen, I had my driver's license and could borrow my father's car when I needed it. Every time my aunt saw me driving off, something disagreeable would happen. I once had a flat tyre on the motorway and was forced to install the spare wheel, trying not to stain my beautiful evening dress. Another time there was this French idiot at a party who jokingly tripped me up, making me fall. I spent the next three weeks with an ankle in a cast. After several similar incidents, even my father began to believe in my aunt's destructive power.

So the 'gris gris' period began; Therese was adamant that she had to protect me. She initiated me in some magical rituals, most of them quite funny, which she said would drive away any negative energy from me. I had to spit seven times over my left shoulder whenever I left the house. I had to cross my fingers behind my back every time my aunt saw me. My nanny loved me like her own child; she never stopped telling me that I was an angel who fell from the sky. Therese's African magic was harmless; she just wanted to do me good. One time I discovered a red pepper that she had hidden in my school bag with a medal of the Virgin Mary attached to it. I loved this chaotic mixture of prayers, coming from different worlds. I was devoted to the Virgin Mary myself, because I had spent all my school time in a convent with Irish nuns. I prayed endlessly, desperately, like a drowning person clinging to a branch for survival.

Years after I left the island, Aunt Clothilde told my cousin Josephine that she felt sorry for the animosity, which existed between her and me. It was my mother's fault, she said. I realised then that all the hate of her and my mother really existed, it was not only the fruit of an adolescent's imagination. These women did not love me, they did not want me to be part of their 'tribe', and they were aware of doing me wrong. But what could I have done to change their feelings? You cannot force anybody to love you.

Chapter 3

In the third house lived Aunt Juliet and her family. On their side, the garden was narrow, designed in immaculate rows and squares. The lawn at the front gave a respectable impression. Geraniums had been planted beside the garage and on the path leading to the house. There were many violets in pots, placed in the shade near the washhouse, an open shed where the housemaid did the washing. A bougainvillea hid the trash corner. Orchids and thick ferns in coloured flower pots, were placed around the house and the sheds. There was a bench under the old avocado tree with shiny leaves. Nature in that part of the garden seemed imprisoned, kept under Aunt Juliet' s control.

The house smelt of wax, and the floor shone like a mirror. Aunt Juliet was a very conscientious house-keeper and she worked all day long. She asked a lot from her small, thin body; she was a bundle of nerves. From the pink light of dawn 'till sunset, she cleaned her cupboards and wardrobes in a frenzy. She had a house-maid whom she watched carefully, writing down her ins and outs. In my aunt's eyes, the maid never seemed to do her job properly. We could hear her grumbling behind the poor woman's back, inspecting each piece of furniture, always finding some dust left. Aunt Juliet would frown and make faces; she was a grumpy woman whom I feared and loved at once, because she took care of me when I was small, sometimes more than my own mother. When she finished her housework in the afternoon, Juliet sat at her sewing table. From there, like a matron, she had a good view over the whole household. Children had to ask for permission before entering any room of the house. I liked to pay a visit to her son to show him the books that I had bought, but first I had to tell my aunt the purpose of my visit. She let me go, often giving me the impression that I was in the way. Juliet's whole hope was focused on this son of hers, Valentin. A loner, shy to the extreme, Valentin was the ideal of a son, a rare specimen. He spent his life studying alone in his ivory tower. He aspired to go to university overseas, but when it was time, his mother made a scene, refusing to let him go. The bird was not allowed to leave its nest. Valentin took courses per correspondence and spent some time at the university of the island, and he climbed up the grades in a renowned company. Even his lack of charisma and his shyness did not prevent him from reaching top management. Valentin never left his mother's home, and always felt responsible for the wellbeing of his family. This was because his sister Josephine became very ill with psoriasis when he was an adolescent. Seeing her so sick, sometimes unable to attend school for weeks, even unable to close her eyes properly while she slept, Valentin expressed a wish to become a priest. He thought of offering his life to God in the hope that this would lead to his sister's healing. The whole family, including his father, the bigot, was so proud of Valentin. They considered him a saint. But then my father, with both his feet on the ground, stopped them all in their hysteria. He made the young man change his mind. This, of course, caused many disputes, my father being the bad one as usual, but he did not care. Josephine found her health after all, with the help of modern medicine and just after falling in love. But years passed by. Valentin, the eternal bachelor, always remained a moral and financial support to his sister. He shared her misery when her children caused her so many tears.

When I was a child, I went to primary school with Aunt Juliet, because she was working there as a teacher. During school holidays, I spent most of the time at her place because both my parents were at work. Aunt Juliet had a bad habit of asking me to solve arithmetic problems or to spell words in French and English at the most inappropriate moments. I was at her mercy; any hesitation or stammering on my part would cause sarcastic comments from her family. Valentin and Josephine, who were at least fifteen years older than me, would have a good laugh, making fun of me. In their world, it was normal to laugh at other people's expense. They did not think much of my intellectual capacities. Sometimes I felt like a real idiot in front of them, and I behaved like one. Luckily this all stopped as soon as I went to high school, where my teachers had a high opinion of me and gave me back my confidence.

When I had finished my A levels, however, and was waiting anxiously for the results, I heard Aunt Juliet saying to her daughter that I had surely failed. She was mentioning all the mistakes I once made in a French dictation in second grade! Since then, the woman had not changed her mind about me, even though I had spent all these years in one of the best schools on the island.

Aunt Clothilde was at my house when I called my mum from school to announce my good results. She turned her back on my mum and hurriedly left the house. My mother saw that her wicked sister had tears of rage and jealousy in her eyes. The beast never congratulated me and stayed hidden in her hole for some days; she could not bear to hear about my success.

My mother said that she preferred her work to home, and chose to stay at the hospital until late. She was not really concerned about her family's wellbeing. Instead of being by myself at home, I developed the habit of spending a lot of time at Aunt Juliet's, following my cousin Josephine's every step like a little dog. Josephine was like a big sister; I liked the way she laughed, she was full of life and so bubbly. But later, her life became more and more difficult, with the worries and disappointments caused by two of her children. I saw her change into an envious woman. She married the first man she ever met, put under pressure because our other cousin, Aunt Clothilde's only daughter, had married at eighteen. Everybody thought that Josephine's fiancé was not of her social rank. My father, intransigent, refused to go to the wedding. My mother decided to go and stood up to him. While we were getting dressed up, my father went on shouting at my mother that her relatives were mixing with the flunkeys, '*la valetaille*', and that my brother and I, his children, his own flesh and blood, would end up the same way, marrying one of them. Our regular taxi came to fetch us and I remember sitting at the rear, looking fearfully at my father's silhouette, the menacing shape of a buffalo, ready to charge. But luckily the taxi drove off and my mother just murmured: "Your dad is a killjoy."

She was right. But my brother and I were delighted at Josephine's marriage with Clement. He was the perfect man. The features of his face were strong, he had a generous smile with beautiful white teeth and he kept his straight black hair relatively long. He was the only adult I knew who was not at all authoritative, and I adored him because of that. Clement was the headmaster of a school, but an artist in his soul. He liked to work with his hands, sculpting and painting at a slow pace. He loved to tell us stories of haunted houses and garden gnomes. We listened to him for hours, opened-mouthed, watching him sculpt, handling the clay with strength and precision until, slowly, a statue was formed; the same image he had previously drawn with charcoal on a canvas. Clement was a gentle, sensitive man, always in a good mood. He saw soon enough that I lived in my own dream world, full of fantasy. I told him about the bright colours in my dreams and he always encouraged me in my forbidden passion: the dance. Josephine was always keen to join us for any entertainment. She had this childish side of hers that I was so fond of. She was still eager to play hide and seek with me, even after her marriage. She was only twenty years old at that time, and I was five. Years later we spent all those summer days together, playing the guitar, singing the same songs over and over again. But this youthful happiness was ephemeral, lasting only until the birth of their children; then it completely disappeared.

In Aunt Juliet's garden there was an unused shed. Clement transformed it into a workshop. This became his shelter, enabling him to escape from his screaming children and from his scolding mother-in-law. Poor Clement, he spent his weekends and the endless holidays in his workshop. He could not get rid of anything, and stored a lot of junk there. That was not to Aunt Juliet's taste at all. Taking advantage of his absence, his mother-in-law used to rush into the workshop and take out any bits and pieces she could get hold of and throw them with rage into the trash. As soon as Clement returned home, the poor chap would retrieve everything from the bin without a word. Then he stayed in his refuge for the rest of the day, offended. He often told my brother and me of his misery, but he never could stand up to his mother-in-law. He called her 'the shrew'.

My parents never invited any friends to our home and I did not dare have anybody visiting me either. My father was so conservative, and had a lot of prejudices; nobody was good enough in his eyes. I was never allowed to pay a visit to any school friend dear to me; invitations to birthday parties were declined categorically. Later on, to avoid an endless discussion with my father, I declined my friends' invitations to their parties myself, without even asking my parents.

That was why I visited my cousins regularly, to see what they were doing. I often caught them in the kitchen, baking cakes, banana fritters or crunchy chilly cakes, just like those that the Indians sold at the market. Their children surrounded them, all excited and loud, while their grandmother Juliet watched from her sewing corner. In the evening, my uncle Marcel, the notary clerk, came back from his office, his face all shiny because of the heat. I knew then that it was time for me to leave. My mother taught me not to disturb them as soon as Juliet's husband came back home.

Juliet revered Marcel. He was the only one whom she seemed to fear, respecting him and never contradicting him. The man could react weirdly when he was upset. Marcel was bald and thin and had a face with prominent cheekbones. He was a hypocrite, and never raised his voice. As soon as he returned home, he withdrew into his living room, a museum of Kitsch, with a sterilized cleanliness. He played the violin there until dinner. He was not a virtuoso, but was good enough to play at church. His life was well ordered; a devoted Catholic, he prayed mornings and evenings, kneeling on his *prie-dieu* in a corner of his bedroom. Aunt Juliet was as devout as he was, and they influenced me a lot. One dark evening, they brought me to light a candle at the grotto of Saint Ignacio, which was in the yard of a monastery. I was a little girl and I was so impressed by this dark hollow, all green with moss, with ivy climbing up its concave walls. Saint Ignacio's naively painted statue seemed gigantic because the dribbling candles lit up the place in such a strange, fascinating way. I believed I met the saint in person, alive. I thought I saw his chest moving gently under his purple robe as if he were breathing. This place was sacred because of this atmosphere of devotion. Silence prevailed; a divine silence.

I felt protected, bathed in the loving energy of the candle-light. The magic continued on the way back home when my uncle Marcel bought me some rice cakes from an Indian woman with a wrinkled face, who was sitting with folded legs on the pavement. Placed in front of her was a small coal stove from which she took a cylinder-shaped cake-tin. She knocked the cover off at one end, and from the other side pushed a long white cake out of the mould. She put the cake on a raffia mat, took a piece of thread from a plastic bag and cut the cake into regular thick slices with the thread. Finally she packed several slices, still hot and smoking, in a piece of paper and gave them to me. As soon as I took some of the cake in my mouth it broke into granules, leaving a taste of slightly sweet rice on my tongue.

I was fond of those special moments with my aunt and uncle; they were so grounded, mixing with real people, showing me how life was outside the realms of my pro-tected world. They did not mind driving along the coast on a public holiday, and taking a break on an over-crowded beach. They went to the horse races at the Champ de Mars and stood shoulder to shoulder with other people. This was their way of life, and my father absolutely disapproved of it. But behind his back I always asked my mother to allow me to go with them, and was absolutely thrilled when I was given permission to do so. Lent was a very special time for them, and for me. All squeezed in Uncle Marcel's small Morris Austin, we drove to every little church on the island. When entering one of these chapels, you first smelled the sea and then the scent of cheap perfume. It came from the devout Creoles sitting nearby, praying with their eyes closed, holding rosaries tightly in their hands. Many of them held their babies in their laps or let them toddle about along the nave. These babies were so lovely, clean and dressed in bright colours; dark cherubs whose joyous babbling created a joyful break in the pious atmosphere.

My childhood and my adolescence were impregnated with holy water and endless prayers. My father was against these Sunday outings. He grumbled about those bigots who swallowed God on Sundays, (he meant the host at Holy Communion) but who spat out the Devil as soon as they left the church with all their gossip and hypocrisy. My father did not believe in the demonstrative devotion of what he called my mother's tribe, and was convinced that even God was exasperated to hear their litanies. I was somewhat shocked by my father's words but not that much, knowing quite well that all the praying and loving of my aunt and uncle were directed to God and his saints, but not really to other human beings. There was a lack of compassion in the family. Nevertheless these day trips were the only way for me to get out of my garden-ghetto.

I learned much of my island at that time, of an extraordinary beauty rich in scents and flavours. In December, the magnificent flamboyants set the landscape on fire with their orange and red flowers. The filaos, or casuarinae, chanted so peacefully when the warm gentle wind blew through their slender, drooping twigs. The sea, of a pure turquoise, broke its waves on black reefs. Hindu women of unreal beauty walked along the roads, undulating their hips with grace. We went for picnics in a hidden bay, and I ran along the beach wearing my red bathing suit, intoxicated by those moments of freedom. I chased tiny white crabs and watched them reversing rapidly into their holes, or I looked for multi-coloured fish in between the pink corals. I was not a good swimmer, so I stayed in the shallow, warm water and let my body float, doing nothing, with my arms stretched out. The adults ate roasted chicken and sandwiches with ham and mustard in the shade. They called me to join them, but I pretended not to hear them, too happy to be in the turquoise water with the sun shining its rays on my body. Too soon, we would have to drive back home through the villages. We saw women washing clothes in the river, with their large skirts turned up above their knees, lather all around them. Naked children played in the water not far from their mothers, shouting cheerfully. In my eyes they were the happiest children in the world.

Often we stopped at a small market. The merchants stood behind their stalls with pyramids of oranges, apples, mangoes and lychees. They sold their goods in an incredible turmoil, everybody trying to bargain. Money passed from hand to hand in a stunning virtuosity. The spices smelled strongly; freshly plucked curry leaves, ginger, saffron, hot pepper, cinnamon, cloves. All these smells tickled my nostrils and suddenly I was famished after spending the whole day at the seaside. Luckily my relatives bought hot samosas and bhajis that young Indian boys cooked on the spot. We walked back to the car, carrying a lot of little bags; we ate the cakes greedily while driving home, burning our fingers.

Those dreadful buses with reckless drivers spoiled the whole idyllic scenery. These people had no sense of danger at all, winding in zigzags on the narrow roads at an infernal speed, using their brakes unwillingly then driving off again abruptly. It was as if they took the passengers for sandbags, jolting them in every direction, putting their lives in danger. Nobody stood up to them. The bus station was situated in the centre of every small town, ruining the whole environment. All the buses were in a dreadful state, spitting a black suffocating smoke, and leaving a streak of soot behind them on the asphalt. The passengers waited for the bus under concrete shelters, so badly built that they left everybody battered in the rain. An awful smell of urine floated in the air, coming from the adjacent toilets that were never cleaned and stayed out of order for months. Men in dirty brownish uniform sold the tickets on the buses, and they treated the passengers roughly. But everybody depended on the public transport because it was affordable, so they stayed passive and seemed not to bother about the pollution and the ugliness surrounding them. During my grandparents' time there were no buses, only the railway. My grandmother used to tell me stories of her youth when she travelled on the steam train to visit relatives all over the country. What a shame that the railway had been abolished, mainly because the owners of the sugar factories preferred trucks with containers to bring sugar to the harbour. Nobody cared about the disastrous consequences for the environment.

Chapter 4

I always went home with a pinch of sadness in my heart. All the joy of the day disappeared as soon as I stepped into the doorway. I did not like my house. It was unfriendly to me, unwelcoming. My parents usually had a row during my absence, so my mother was always in one a terrible mood and I dreaded her. She did not like seeing me all tanned after a whole day in the sun. She screamed at me and called me a Negress. I was slapped in the face, and I would run and shut myself in my bedroom. As usual, my father would withdraw to the kitchen. He spent all his Sundays there trying out new recipes. A bouillabaisse simmered for hours in the pot, under his fatherly supervision, a bottle of whisky keeping him company. When he was in a good mood, he sang a song from an opera; he had a very good voice, a light baritone. But if he was in bad mood, he pestered me about my mother. He always said the same thing, that he should never have married this woman, his mother had warned him, told him that he would regret it but he did not listen to her. He had married beneath his station and this caused him to be rejected from his family and friends. They had all avoided him ever since. My father would go on and on with his story, and

I stayed there, having to listen to his drunkard's speech, these same words hammering my head. How I longed for another life, with peaceful parents! My mother was frustrated in her marriage because my father stopped feeling attracted to her very soon after their marriage; I remember them always sleeping in separate rooms. She spoke about this intimate matter shamelessly, which was quite embarrassing for me. But my mother did not lead an easy life with this man who just criticised everything. He booed the tenor during the opera while seated among all sorts of stiff people, leaving my mother and me dying of embarrassment. If he was invited to a dinner party, he made sarcastic comments about the wine: 'tasteless'; and the food: 'left-overs from the hospital?'

All his relatives, except for one uncle from his mother's side, died in the concentration camps they were sent to during the Second World War. It seemed that my father did not really know who he was, not belonging any-where. Because of his marriage with my mother, who was of mixed race, he lost all contact with his own world. The friends of his youth rejected him without even knowing who my mother really was. They did not know how refined she was; much more educated than the lot of them. My father had a superiority complex, and his arrogance made him enemies, especially at work. His colleagues stayed away from him. He avoided them anyway.

The problem was that, contrary to my brother, Louis, I found myself totally isolated from the rest of the world. But how could I possibly socialise? I was constantly hearing comments about this 'son of a slave', an expression applied to all those that my father disliked for an unknown reason; and there were so many of them in his eyes. There were the others, no doubt, nice chaps, but they belonged to the common people and we should never get to know them, never have them in our house. It was interesting to see that my father had the same way of thinking as his mother, even though he was a victim of her narrow-mindedness. My grandmother never accepted the fact that her son had married a woman of mixed race. She died without ever seeing my mother. It was not surprising that I was unhappy in this whole family, even if I loved everyone deeply. At school, with the nuns, I boasted about how my father was a really good engineer and how my mother was such a great welfare officer, working closely with the psychiatrists and being so appreciated at the hospital. My mother worked with devotion, she was responsible for the reintegration of patients in society. Moreover, she was always keen to stay at the hospital for every party given by the staff. For special celebrations, she was the one in charge of organising the festivities. She was so good at it that she became indispensable for the coordination of all medical conferences taking place at the hospital, or whenever there was an official visit of the governor. She knew all the protocols, and her subordinates appreciated her. My mother was very happy at her workplace because her talents were recognised there. She had this natural elegance and her clothes suited her perfectly. She had narrow hips and generous breasts, and liked to wear big necklaces or earrings with her strict suits. She had a graceful carriage of the head and always sat as upright as an 'i'. She was a very beautiful woman who loved to laugh and have fun whenever she was away from home. But as soon as she was home, she had to face a husband who was jealous of her strong personality and intelligence and humiliated her constantly. My father never complimented her, he saw her only as an emancipated woman whose cooking capacities were mediocre. My mother could live in total chaos. But she gave great attention to hygiene; careful not to spread any bacteria from the hospital. She never allowed us to hug or kiss her when she came back from work. We had to wait until she had taken a shower and changed her clothes. Therese, the nanny, was in charge of the household, but there was a lack of care. I felt bad about it, and envied the houses of my aunts where everything was immaculate. But occasionally, especially around Christmas, my mother would come home with bags full of embroidered Chinese tablecloths, heavy brocade curtains, and porcelain vases which she filled with flowers. In one magical flash she could give an elegant and thriving look to our shabby house.

Our lifestyle was quite different from my aunts', whose only preoccupation was to save as much money as possible. My mother used to buy me the best clothes and my wardrobe made the richest girls I knew green with envy. I had generous pocket money, which I spent at the patisserie near the school, eating millefeuilles and lemon tarts with my friends. My father was very generous to the poor; he always tried to lighten their life, help them pay their doctors' bills or buy good shoes for their children. Food was always in abundance in our house and it was shared with everybody. Our maid, Therese, and Naren, the gardener, were part of the family. We knew a lot about their private lives. We shared their worries and my parents cared for them and their children, buying the necessary schoolbooks. Their weaknesses, especially those of Therese, were largely tolerated. She had the bad habit of not attending work at nearly every end of the month, as soon as she received her wages from my mum. She usually came back a week after, with a guilty expression on her face and with a very empty purse. My mother would reprimand her a little, but soon they would be chatting as old friends again while drinking hot tea.

In a way, my brother and I were brought up in an atmosphere of grandeur. This helped me to feel at ease in the sophisticated places I visited years later as an adult. But it had a bad influence on my brother who later turned out to be very materialistic, marrying an even more materialistic woman and living a luxurious life, beyond his financial capacities.

Christmas was extraordinary at our house. My mother was an extravagant spender and my brother and I received the most beautiful gifts any child would dream of. I think that my mother wanted us to have the toys that she never received as a child. However there was always a sort of electricity in the air, a sort of retained aggressiveness. The joy of Christmas did not last very long. The same evening, it was quite usual that my parents started arguing in an explosion of screams and insults. The child I was never could really enjoy any feeling of happiness, of wellbeing at Christmas, knowing that this feeling could end up abruptly at any moment, when husband and wife would start fighting again.

I had to make myself as invisible as possible. My mother had a habit of taking revenge on me; I would be slapped for nothing if I was within reach. This is why I became quite difficult to deal with during my adolescence, standing up to my mother, snapping at her; but I never stopped longing for her love. I was insecure, scared, and lonely, but I was very proud and had to fight for myself.

Chapter 5

———◆———

Louis, my brother, was my mum's pet. Her one and only! In her eyes, he was the most beautiful, most intelligent and the only one at home who could make her laugh. There was a deep love between the two of them, a real fusion. All others did not count; they got in the way. His birth was a sign of victory after the rejection of her in-laws. She breastfed her son for two years. I was born five years later, when she was already very disappointed with my father's tyrannical behaviour. She did not want another child, but I was conceived accidentally while my parents were cruising towards England on the 'Pierre Loti'. My mother explained the situation very clearly to me on my fourteenth birthday. She told me she did not have an abortion because she could not; she was on a ship. During her pregnancy, my parents and brother stayed for months in England, where my mother felt very lonely. They were there during the winter; my father came late from his work, spending his whole evenings in pubs. She stayed all by herself in a B&B, waiting for her husband to come back. She did everything to get back to the island before giving birth to me. I have a feeling that she did try for an abortion as soon as she was home. There was the story that she had been prescribed a peculiar medicine because the doctor said that her body had retained too much water. That's why I was born with my face covered with wrinkles, like an old woman. Moreover, there is a rumour that my father said at my birth:

'A girl! Give her to the pigs!'

These words have been said and repeated, I do not know how often, by my mother, especially if she saw that I was having a peaceful conversation with my father and she felt unwanted. One day my brother repeated these terrible words to me in front of his wife. He was jealous of me whenever he saw that I felt great and everything was going on well in my life. He wanted me to be the vulnerable sad little girl again. But I stopped him and told him that these words had lost all their power over me. I was grown up now.

Louis grew up with the absolute certitude that he was someone extremely important, absolutely irresistible and that the whole world should throw itself at his feet. He had the beauty of the devil, a charmer with an irresistible smile. He could do anything and my mother would melt under his charm, but this was not enough. My brother had to seduce his whole entourage. He was a chronic liar; he lied for everything, even for little things. He told fabulous stories in which he depicted himself as a hero. He was a real megalomaniac. To tell lies was, for him, totally natural. Even as an adult, he stayed in his world of lies; I think this made him feel happy. But far more than that, his selfishness made him manipulate people without the least feeling of guilt.

During his childhood Louis behaved quite aggressively towards me, especially when my father was away. My mother was always on my brother's side, scolding me when I cried because he used force to take my things. My mother always said that I was making a fuss about nothing. She told me it was his way of showing me that he liked me. She did not bother when he took my books to give to his girlfriend, or broke my new watch with a sick pleasure. What was awful for me was that my brother was cruel to our pets. The dog kept away from him, afraid to be kicked. Louis kept birds in a cage, beautiful Bengalis with red beaks. He did not really take care of them. I watched them everyday; little innocent victims kept in a cage. Luckily Louis soon enough lost interest in keeping them. One day, at last, I saw him carry the cage outdoors and shake it to let the birds fly away. To avoid the anger of our father, Louis accused me of having opened the cage during his absence. I was so relieved for the little birds that I did not say a word to defend myself. My father believed him because I always wanted the birds to be freed but he did not reprimand me. My brother's misbehaviour, first at primary school, then at high school, did not alter my mother' s total confidence in him in the least. But my father did not share the same fad for his son at all. Indeed he was very hard on him. So hard that it hurt me, I felt pity for my brother.

The real trouble started when Louis turned seventeen. Friends took on a vital role in his life and he scarcely came home, only to eat and get changed. He had made friends with some dodgy young men, brothers, musicians in a band who played on Saturdays in a nightclub that was supposedly en vogue. We felt that he was drifting away. Of course my mother kept her worries to herself; she had to protect him from my father's anger. But from her comportment, I knew that she was in great fear for her son. I think that Louis had started taking drugs; he was so skinny and his lips were swollen. More than once, my mother went to these people's house and forced my brother to come home. Like a tigress defending her cub, my mother fought body and soul to free her son from the negative influence of these people. Finally she threatened the young men's mother that she would call the police if my brother ever went there again. This was the right thing to say. Louis ended his relationship with this family after that, and he seemed to have stopped taking drugs just in time.

Louis finished school in a rather chaotic way. He had no respect for any teacher and showed no interest in his studies; he even made fun of the president of the national broadcasting corporation, calling him a fat cat on the school premises. My mother had to write a letter of apology on his behalf. Soon he was thrown out of his private school, and after that he was sent to several other schools, but he always kept his arrogant attitude towards the teachers. My parents were devastated. Louis was so intelligent; how could he have fallen so low! Unfortunately for me, my father compared me to my brother and he told Louis constantly to follow my path and spend some of his time in his books. Convinced that my father loved me more than him, Louis started to hate me, humiliating me in front of his friends when they came to visit him. He would point at me and tell them to look at this idiot who has only got a dog as a friend! He would go on and on. criticising everything about me, that I had an ugly nose, just like her father, this stupid bastard! The boys all found it very funny indeed and laughed heartily at my brother's jokes, while looting the fridge.

Chapter 6

I continued doing my best at school, trying hard not to be a burden to my parents. I was looking for a word of acknowledgement from my mother, but it was in vain. My studies and my state of mind did not preoccupy my mother at all. So I grew up all by myself, going through the turpitudes of my adolescence in absolute independence. Luckily, at school I had sincere friends in whom I could confide. I still think of my friend Gianella, a wonderful girl, extremely intelligent, who lived with a very dominant mother; very ambitious and quite frightening. We lived not far away from each other, and took the bus back home together every day. We used to laugh a lot. She took violin lessons with an old gentleman who lived in a small house full of plants and cats. I waited for her at her teacher's house and we took the bus back home afterwards, talking about music, about love. We fell in love, platonically of course, with the same boy, without feeling the least jealous of each other. We knew that we were only playing as if we were in love. She was like a sister, but I lost touch with her as soon we finished school; her mother was too annoying. She asked me once if I was a moth attracted to her daughter's light! From that day I decided not to go back to my friend's house anymore. Gianella left the country shortly afterwards to continue her studies at university in the United Kingdom. I never saw her again.

While my mother was giving her whole attention to my brother, someone told her that my father had a mistress, a Chinese girl with the fat and smooth body of a penguin, who lived not far away from us. My father had been seen leaving the woman's house very late in the evening. When my mother heard about it, she exploded with anger, like an erupting volcano. She spat all her hate towards my father, day and night. This was hell for him, for me, for everyone in the house. My mother woke up at night and started insulting my father, screaming at him, waking everybody. She did not cry, she screamed. At night, when my father went for a walk, she followed him and she urged me to come with her. We hid behind fences, walked bent over from bush to bush, trying to see whether my father was going to meet his mistress. I was angry with my father for humiliating my mother by betraying her, and even worse, with someone living down our street. I am sure that what he did led to my mother's madness. She had always been emotionally on the edge, often behaving very strangely. But her husband's cheating on her confirmed that he did not love her at all. It was too much for my mother, who sank in the abyss. Poor Mum, I did feel for her. This marriage brought her nothing but humiliation and suffering.

One night, after one of those horrible scenes full of insults and screams, my father decided to leave the house. He packed his personal things and left. That night I fell into a deep sleep without dreams; an appeasing blackness. The next day I went to school without saying a word to my mother. I was relieved and was already deciding whether I should stay with my mother or go and live with my father. But that same evening my father returned home like a coward, sat in his red armchair and began to drink his whisky. When he was drunk, I heard him saying to himself how his life was a real curse. But my mother must have been very scared. There were no hysterical screams to be heard anymore. This whole affair brought a lot of excitement to the lives of my aunts. They were too happy to be able to talk negatively about my father, enjoying my mother's misery, commenting on it all for months.

I continued to live a life without trouble; or rather I lived trying not to cause any trouble. I went to school light-heartedly, because school was my oasis. There I could be myself; a sensible young girl. The teachers liked me and trusted me. My classmates voted for me nearly every year as class captain. I loved the atmosphere of the convent, with the nuns singing so beautifully every morning at the chapel. I liked the huge park with its camphor laurels surrounding the school buildings. During winter, the rain fell persistently, keeping us company day after day on our way to school. But the rain had the sweet taste of serenity; I knew that I would be at peace emotionally for the whole day. A dog freed from its chain must have felt the same way. My friends were all charming; all so different from each other; of different races, different social classes, and different religions. It did not matter in the least; we were all wearing the school uniform and we were not allowed to wear any jewellery. It was such an interesting experience for us girls, to grow up together. We shared the problems that we encountered at home. We all had our dreams and hopes, and despite our different cultures we were all the same naive young girls believing that we would achieve more goals than our mothers. We thought we would change the world as soon as we finished high school.

On my seventeenth birthday, my mother looked at me intensively from head to toe. People used to say that I had the smile of an angel. Not my mother. She thought I was fat, with hanging buttocks. I apparently did not stand upright, and she thought I had this strange sort of lump on my right hip. She called me 'the tortoise' because in her eyes, I pulled my neck forward when I was watching television. Worse, in her mind I breathed too loudly; she used to pinch me whenever I brought my face towards hers to say something to her. Sometimes I held my breath while she came near me. To correct my posture, she would give me a slap under the chin or on the hips at any time, in front of everybody. She even hated the colour of my skin, but she was much darker than I was. One day she brought me a lightening cream from South Africa. I had to use it, she said. Some days later my face turned as red as a cooked lobster. Then came the pimples, which became pustules, and later they became a thick black crust over my whole face. I was unrecognisable, walking with my head bent, hiding. The joy of going to school disappeared from one day to the next. I looked at my friends, so beautiful and happy, and I cried. My friends were sad for me, they knew about my mother and thought she had succeeded in destroying me. My mother became exultant and told me that it was God's hand. He had punished me. Why? What had I done wrong? I believed in my mother's words, I was convinced God had punished me for what I was. I had to believe in this woman's words - after all, she was my mother. My nanny, Therese, the old woman with a wrinkled face, my beloved witch, opened her toothless mouth and begged my mother to take me to a dermatologist. The doctor shouted at my mother: how could she give me such a dangerous cream. My young sensitive skin had reacted badly, developing an 'acnea vulgaris'. I suffered from acne for many years afterwards. I still have the scars on my face, and when I look in the mirror I have to think of my mother. She succeeded in transforming a beautiful, perfect face into a minefield just because she did not love me, her only daughter. Maybe she did love me, but wanted to change my appearance into her ideal of beauty and perfection. She would rather change my personality as well, bend me like melting glass, and take possession of my soul. Was she jealous of my youth, of my femininity? Yes she was, I feel quite certain about that. For years after that, she reminded me of God's punishment. Victorious at any lack of obedience from my part, she would tell me to look at my face in the mirror and insistently ask me whether the punishment was not enough; if I had to feel God's hand again. This woman was so strong, so devilish and I was her daughter that could not do anything to get loose from her claws. But I was a fighter; I perked up just to show her. I examined myself and found that apart from my skin, I was a beautiful girl. I had big dark brown eyes and long lashes, a beautiful smile and perfect white teeth. I had a perfect body, now very slim and muscular because I was practicing a lot of sport and yoga and had lost my teenage superfluous kilos. In spite of my mother's criticism, I always walked upright with my head held high. It did not matter that I had some scars on my face, I was beautiful and nobody could think the opposite. I learned to use make-up to cover the worst. In fact my boyfriends did not even notice the scars on my face. Funnily they would only be noticed by girls and later, women who were jealous of me.

Chapter 7

My mother never forgot that my brother was in a difficult situation and needed help. Thanks to her good connections at work, she succeeded in finding him a job in a
bank. All of a sudden, Louis put an end to his misbehaviour. From that point on, he became more interested
in the 'weaker' sex and other nice worldly things. He
started seeking the company of people who could, in
one way or another, bring some benefit. There was a
complete metamorphosis in his personality, the young
'good-for-nothing' had become an arriviste; ready to do
anything to have his dreams come true.

My brother used to go out with several girls at a time
and usually let them down very easily. But he did keep
one of them, going out with her on and off while still
flirting with somebody else. This girl had dark blonde
hair and grey eyes. Her name was Shirley; she was petite
and her bum was not bigger than two apples. After
some time, Shirley's father, clever as a fox, invited my
brother to his house. He did not want his daughter to
hang around in the streets with a boy. As soon as my
brother stepped into Shirley's house, his relationship
with her was made quasi-official. Shirley was finally

invited to our place as well, rather reluctantly and after quite a lapse of time, following the insistence of my brother. From the very first moment she arrived, she destabilised my parents, taking power over them, even though she was a very quiet person. My mother lost all her confidence in front of this tiny young woman. Even my cynical father tried to tame her. This girl was very distrustful towards our family. Until that time I had grown up with exuberant and talkative girls who knew how to engage in a conversation with anybody. But Shirley did not talk. She was incapable of completing any sentence, answering by onomatopoeia, nearly inaudible, or with only 'yes' or 'no'. She had an irritating habit of repeating your questions while her grey eyes would express a total nothingness, as if asking herself if she really had to answer. So to put an end to the embarrassing situation, someone else would speak for her; she then only had to nod her head. When my father at last succeeded in having her talk to him, he could not stop telling us about it, as if this were a real sensation. He also noticed that her French was not very fluent; her family seemed to speak the patois creole at home. How disappointing for my parents when they realised that the girl with white skin was not as refined as they had wished. Shirley put her hand in front of her mouth when she smiled, like a geisha. She had to hide her teeth, which were surprisingly askew and greenish; quite unpleasant to look at. But everybody focused on her white skin and grey eyes and everybody was delighted; a European appearance was very popular in the tropics. One day I had a strange feeling while looking at her somewhat distorted mouth. She was trying to smile while pressing her lips together. Was she trying to hide her mouth because it was a chasm, the opening to a wicked soul? I did not know yet how intuitive I was.

Soon enough, I noticed that my brother was constantly lost in his own thoughts, which was not really his nature. I knew he was planning something. Then came the day when he told my father about a dream house which would be the perfect home for our family. He talked about it for weeks and weeks, convincing my father that the house would be a getaway from my mother's relatives. Louis showed the small jewel to my father. They met the vendor and my father finally agreed to buy the house. But at the solicitor's office Louis, taking my father by surprise, insisted that the house should be in his name. What a 'coup de poker'! Later on, my father said he was forced to agree because of my mother's insistent plea at the attorney's office. Apparently she was acting like a tigress, urging him to give the house to my brother. It was clear that my mother and my brother had planned it all beforehand. My father had been fooled. Louis's next step was to manipulate his father-in-law-to-be in order to obtain a brand new car. That did the trick; Louis had succeeded in acquiring everything he needed effortlessly. The planning for the wedding of the century could begin.

Meanwhile I was working hard at school, aspiring to study overseas after my graduation. I wanted to become a journalist or a lawyer. But my parents did not even think of being empathetic towards me during the preparations for the exams. In the evenings, my father drank and talked nonsense while my mother argued with him. It was impossible to study. However good my results, the competition had been better and a scholarship was as improbable as winning the lottery. My dream fell to pieces. The little exotic bird had its wings tied up; it would not be flying away to freedom. Not yet. When I complained about not being able to obtain a scholarship for studying at university, my father stayed cold-hearted and did not think of paying for my studies, even if he had enough money. He did not intend to let me go anywhere. He wanted to keep me under his control, too afraid to see me living my life as I wanted. I had started to have a conflicted relationship with him as soon as I became a young adult. He could not stand it when young men looked at me. He looked back at them men-acingly, and walking beside him in public was really unpleasant. When we attended parties, which we very rarely did, he watched me intensely every time I danced with someone. If my dance partner started to talk to me, my father would call me severely and the scared young man would immediately move away. My mother, who was obsessed with sex, said that my father's behaviour proved that he was a pervert and that he had dirty thoughts about me. My father was neither a pervert, nor did he have dirty thoughts about me, but he was certainly very possessive and jealous. So jealous that he changed towards me, his beloved daughter. He, whom I trusted the most in the family, who protected me from a hateful mother, suddenly stopped being my ally. He became hard and nasty as soon as I wanted to be inde-pendent. He made me feel insecure with his sarcastic comments about me. When I pointed out that I wished to have my own children one day, he replied with a dismissive wave of the hand that he did not care, as these children would not bear his name. This showed me quite clearly that my father could not accept that one day I would fall in love and have a family. What a paternal love indeed. I always wondered why my soul chose to have these individuals as parents.

Realising that I could not go to university was a cruel fall to harsh reality, but I did not waste time in self-pity. I took my life in my own hands. I began to apply for jobs while taking courses in accountancy and typing, which was the most boring thing for me to do. At that time, it was very hard to find a job on the island. I could feel how relieved my father was when I returned home after each unsuccessful interview. He did not say a word. There was nothing but an absolute silence on his part that reflected how much he feared seeing me acquire any kind of freedom. But this time, my mother was on my side. She used her connections and asked them for recommendations, but none of them had a job for me. When I started talking about journalism, my brother pulled a face; he talked me out of it and said that this job was very badly remunerated. He added that I was living on a cloud; how could I think of such a stupid job that had no opportunities at all on the island. I do not know why, but I believed in this know-all and decided to let go of one of my dearest dreams. Finally I went to see a job-hunter, the mother of a school friend. She gave me special attention, thanks to her daughter. A few weeks later, I was surprised to have a job in an insurance company. I was so proud to have found the job all by myself. It was definitely not on my wish list, but who cared? Back home, my mother showed relief whereas my father seemed rather upset. But I was happy and excited; it had taken me nine months to find this job. This was the first step to my independence.

Chapter 8

My office was in a building of the seventies, a bloc of red bricks with huge tinted windows. The ground floor was a spacious hall; a wooden counter separated the customers from the underwriters. Some screens and green plants placed here and there gave some privacy to the personnel. Everybody worked close to one another, the secretaries, the girls in the typing pool and the insurance agents. The directors and managers had their office at the back of the building. They had flower arrangements on all the furniture in every corner of the room, and this created a ridiculously hushed ambiance. I would be working in the palpitating atmosphere of this microcosm for the next five years. I had to fight for my dreams and I never surrendered, never let myself be drawn away by the surrounding mediocrity, like so many of the young and talented people around me.

The first few months I had to work in the accountancy department. It was a real nightmare. From nine o'clock in the morning till late afternoon, I was confined in a small office at the end of a dark corridor. I shared this claustrophobic room with two other women, who were terribly unfriendly to me because they did not want any stranger to disturb them in their intimacy; they had been working together for more than twenty years. Mary Rose, the more dreadful of the two, was extremely unattractive; she had an excessively protruding chin. Nevertheless she had succeeded in finding a husband. Married to an engineer, she still could not believe that this man had been attracted to her, even if she was ugly from head to toe. I think she pinched herself every morning when she saw him lying beside her in bed. Every Monday I heard her relating to her friend a detailed account of her romantic weekend, spent with her dear husband. Mary Rose had a stronger personality than her colleague, Maria, which was pronounced 'Maaria' (this distortion of the r's was part of the peculiar accent used by the white people of the island). Maria was a grey mouse; tiny, blond with blue eyes; she spoke with a disagreeable nasal twang. It seemed as though every word she would say was dragged along. She hid her hypocrisy under a fragile appearance. Very manipulative, she was always pushing Mary Rose to say something nasty to the other colleagues. Mary Rose and Maria had no secrets from each other; they talked about everything: the meals they wanted to prepare for dinner, the issues they had with their mothers-in-law, and of course about every colleague's private life. They called home regularly for a quick check, making sure that their housemaids were still working. The accountant, a fat man and somewhat coarse, was very fond of these two women because, despite their nastiness, they were doing a really good job; they were like two efficient counting machines. I was a novice, quite slow, but of good will. But the two women did not give me a chance. I heard Mary Rose complaining about me to the accountant; they wanted to get rid of me. Luckily for me, he turned a deaf ear and was very patient and nice to me. As these women were constantly whispering things and giggling behind my back, I lost confidence in myself, and went to work with a heavy heart. Their behaviour flashed me back into my childhood, back in my grand-mother's kitchen surrounded by my aunts, all listening to my mother who, pointing her finger at me, was telling them what a naughty girl I was. But I had no choice, so I continued to go to work. Polite but distant, I did my job, hoping for the wicked women to get tired of bullying me.

After three months I heard there was a vacancy at the typing pool. I went to see the personnel manager and asked him if I could have the job. He said yes, even though I told him I was just a beginner at typing. The next week I got rid of those two women. With victory in my heart, I looked at their bewildered faces. What a joy not to have to deal with numbers and money all day long!

It was an everyday fight with the typewriter, but I worked very hard and I found myself a new talent; I could organise things really well, and my new col-leagues were grateful. I was surrounded by female typists but also by friendly young men, the underwriters, who were very fond of me. The atmosphere at work was much better now. We were laughing a lot. Everything was going better for me; I was having fun in my job.

Chapter 9

Meanwhile, my brother was very busy preparing his wedding with his blonde fiancée. She seemed to focus all her attention on the ceremony; no thoughts were lost on the implications of marriage in itself. Shirley continued to ignore us stubbornly; she really did not hide her reluctance to come to our home. It was evident that my brother had to force her to visit my parents.

Finally the wedding ceremony took place. The bride looked beautiful, the groom radiant, the guests had been meticulously chosen; the richer the better. I found myself in front of the altar as the maid of honour. What a surprise! I suppose that being my brother's only sibling; they had no choice but to give me that task. I stood behind the groom like a movie extra and smiled for the photographs. My mother was trying to hide her tears during the whole ceremony, but her sadness was immense. She was losing the only love of her life.

At the beginning of their marriage, it seemed to me that Louis and Shirley were really attracted to each other. Shirley was obviously using her sexuality as a means to be spoiled by her husband. Louis granted her all her wishes. He always woke up earlier than her in the morning and brought her a cup of tea in bed after he cleaned the kitchen. But Louis could not live without seeing his mother, so every morning he would just pop in at our place before going to his work. His wife waited for him in the car, refusing to come in to say hello. My mother found her behaviour quite shocking, but went out personally every time to invite her for a cup of tea. Finally the witch would get out of the car, dragging her feet, her lips held tight; she refused to say a word to any of us. Often she looked as if she had just got out from under her bed sheets; her eyes still swollen from sleep. She seemed to have stayed in bed until the last minute and got dressed as quickly as possible without washing herself. Our doubts were confirmed when one day we heard Louis asking her if she had 'at least brushed her teeth'. What a shame for a woman to be asked such a question by her newly wed husband. My mother and I kept it to ourselves, but soon enough, my father started to comment about Shirley's untidy appearance. He talked about it to my brother, and Louis reacted very aggressively; he screamed at my father and insulted him. He never let anybody say anything negative about his wife.

After the birth of their daughter about two years later, one could see that their relationship had changed. The physical attraction disappeared, leaving nothing exciting between these two immature individuals but the joy of partying and living a materialistic life. Years later, Shirley told me that after the birth of the baby, Louis focused totally on being a father and more or less ignored her. My brother, on the other hand, confided in me that he was very disappointed to have a wife who spent her weekends in bed. Shirley woke up very late, and after lunch she had to lie down and sleep again. So my brother started to leave his wife at home to go here and there, visiting his numerous friends. My father used to call Louis the 'wandering Jew', because he could not stay put at home. I think that it was not easy for Shirley to be married to my brother, but she also had her faults. She was the laziest person I ever knew. Worse, she was a sly person and began a very active extramarital sexual life. People started to gossip; one had seen her in town walking hand in hand with another man, another saw her in a bus with someone else some time after. My brother thought that she was taking tennis lessons or playing volleyball after work. She seemed to have love affairs with different men, and while she was having a good time, my mother was caring for her baby. Her mother used to tell my parents that she got married 'far too young' at twenty-one, and she could not be bothered with her household and her family. Listening to her, you would think that my parents had forced her daughter to get married. Shirley did not feel the need to learn how to cook, nor iron, nor take care of her household. She was convinced that everybody else should do the work for her.

After Shirley gave birth to their baby, my brother decided to bring her and the baby to our place so that my mother could take care of them. They stayed in our house for three whole months. Without even asking, my mother gave my bedroom to them. I had to sleep in the tiny spare room on a sofa, and my personal belongings were scattered all around the house. Evenings, after work, it was impossible to relax anymore with a good book. Nor did I have a corner where I could practice yoga. Shirley's friends and innumerable relatives were frequent visitors to the house, especially in the evenings; the grandmother, the aunts, the cousins who came to pay a visit to the newly born. These people were noisy and they invaded our privacy shamelessly. I greeted them politely and then I tried to make myself as invisible as possible. But of course, the comments started flowing out of their ugly mouths; I seemed to be so indifferent to the baby. Shirley's grandmother asked me: "Why don't you like babies?"

These women jumped so readily to conclusions. I tried to defend myself as well as I could, because I loved babies and I found my little niece adorable. I suppose that dear Shirley must have told them that I was not the type to change the baby's nappies. Why should I? My mother and all the other women were doing it anyway. I thought it was time for Shirley to grow up and take care of her own child. She stayed in bed for so many weeks, doing nothing but breastfeeding; everything else was being taken care of for her. My poor mother and my nanny were doing all the washing and cleaning for the whole family, not to forget my father who was doing the cooking and making sure that the visitors had something to eat as well. Nonetheless, Shirley continued to hate us. It hurt my mother to see the reaction of Shirley's relatives; when she entered the bedroom everybody hushed. It was quite evident that Shirley was complaining about us.

I was getting fed up with not having any privacy when, three months later, Louis decided to spend some time at the seaside with his family. One of Shirley's uncles invited them to his house on the beach. I started to feel at home again when, three weeks later, he called me and asked me to fetch them in the car he had left at our place. The car refused to start; probably the battery was flat because it had not been used for quite a long time. I tried my best but it did not work. My father was scathing: "Your brother should solve his problem himself."

I asked my cousin Clement for help; he was not very good with cars and he could not help me. I decided to take my father's car and, together with my mother, we drove off to meet my brother. It was a good two hours' drive from home, but when my brother saw us in my father's car, instead of greeting us, he became really infuriated and called me all sorts of names; slut, prostitute, worthless negress! He just could not stop insulting me.

"Who does she think she is? She thinks she is better than me because of her worthless Baccalaureate certificate and her studies as an insurance broker. She is so arrogant, acting as if she is an intellectual, always a book in her hands. No wonder not a man is interested in her."

He screamed so much that even my mother, who was usually on his side, was really shocked. She was well aware of all my efforts to start his stupid car. But what annoyed me most was to see how Shirley reacted to her husband's behaviour. She did not open her mouth, she did not try to calm him; she had this triumphant look that I would often see. She rejoiced that my brother was humiliating me. I did not see the point of spitting so much hate in my face; it had nothing to do with not bringing his car. This was just an opportunity for my brother to pull me down in front of his wife, as if under a spell. After that he went off and withdrew in the house for the whole day, leaving my mother and I outside without anything to drink or eat. We spent the day at the beach under the burning sun. Shirley stayed in the house with him. Then in the late afternoon, we saw them coming out of the house and they packed their things into the car. Without a word, we squeezed in on the back seat with all their things and the baby. Today, I ask myself why I did not drive back home with my mother, leaving him and his family where they were. However when we had passed the entrance gate of our garden I had the courage to say, clearly and firmly:

"As of today, I am taking my own bedroom back."

My brother went to see his car. We could hear him cursing and saying horrible things about me again. He pretended, after an hour, that he had started the car without the faintest difficulty. They immediately started off to Shirley's parents' home and stayed there for a year or so.

After being badly treated by my brother, I kept even more distance from them, preferring to make friends with some of my colleagues. Most of us were still single and very young. One day they all invited me to go dancing with them on a Friday night. I panicked. How would I tell them that my father did not allow me to go out? After reflecting about it, I decided to take action; this had to end. The next Friday came; I told my mother that I was going out. I got dressed and waited patiently for one of the boys to come and pick me up. When he came, I just walked up to the door and said good-bye joyously to my parents. Of course my father asked me where I was going, so I replied:

"Dad, I am going dancing with my colleagues."

Before he had time to say a word, I hurried to the car and off I went, to spend one of the best nights of my life, dancing till dawn! I imposed this new situation on my father and continued to go dancing every Friday, even if I had to hear all kinds of reprimands. He also liked to shout:

"As long as you live in this house you have to do as I say."

But I paid no heed to his screams and did as I pleased. In fact, there was not another girl as well behaved as I was. I never started to date any of my colleagues and made sure to not let myself get into strange situations, so I could stay very good friends with all my colleagues. I loved to dance and was so happy to be able to do so. It was really worth the pain of having to confront that monster of a father who was waiting for me at home.

Chapter 10

One day Catherine, a friend but not a very close one, asked me to join her on a trip to the Seychelles. We could stay with a friend of hers. But Catherine did not have enough money to pay for the flight, and of course I told her that I would pay for her. I planned excitedly for the trip, not knowing that this would bring a total change to my life.

After some weeks we finally took a plane to the Seychelles. My mother took me to the airport, and I remember how annoyed I was with her because she did not stop telling me to try to meet a nice boyfriend. At that time, I had just started dating a very attractive young man, but of course my parents disapproved of him. After some months, however, I had to admit that my boyfriend was a gambler and quite possessive. After some fights and some tears on my part, I decided to put an end to the relationship.

Mahe was a colourful island, heaven on earth. Our hosts' house was built in colonial style; entirely wooden, with a grey roof. There was a bougainvillea climbing up the pillars of the verandah. There was a strong smell of wax as we entered the house and a little housemaid, still a child, was polishing the floor with a brush that was nothing but the fibered husk of a coconut cut in half. Catherine's friend was called Marlene; she was in her fifties and her husband, Antoine – a small skinny man – immediately got on very well with me. They were the stressed parents of three sons and two daughters. One of the girls, Cecile, was about to get married and we were invited to the wedding. The eldest son, Louis, had sex with one of their maids and she got pregnant. He kept it secret until the day that the maid paid a visit to his parents. She was holding a baby in her arms and told them that this little boy was their grandchild, Louis', son. She gave the baby to Marlene and off she went, never to come back. From that day, the boy grew up in the family, surrounded by a loving father and affectionate grandparents. All this was done in the simplest way, without fuss. I was quite impressed by the broad-mindedness of these people. What a joy to live a life without taboos!

Our first night on the island was quite strange and agitated, because just outside our bedroom was a huge breadfruit tree. Two to three times, one of these heavy fruits fell on the corrugated iron roof, causing a tremendous noise. Catherine woke up terrified each time it happened. I spent the night murmuring to her: "It's only a breadfruit."

I just wanted to calm her down. But the next morning she made fun of me, telling everybody that I was in a sort of trance during the whole night. She had been behaving very nervously even during the flight, jumping at the slightest thing and asking too many stupid questions of the steward. As I said before, I did not know her very well, and had the strange feeling that she was seeking attention and could be difficult to deal with.

Marlene's eldest sons were about our age. After work they played in a band and when, on the next Saturday night, they had to perform in a club, they asked us to be their background singers. This was a crazy experience for me. There I was, holding the microphone like a pro, singing in duo with one of the brothers, proud of the applause of the public that consisted mainly of locals. It was the first time in my life that I had done something I liked without the faintest feeling of guilt or fear. I had my first taste of freedom and it was exhilarating. This small interlude intensified my wish to get out of my family ghetto.

Then came the day of Cecile's wedding and Catherine and I helped in the preparations. Early in the morning we went to the church and joined friends of the family who had brought huge amounts of white flowers. We decorated the altar and the nave, and the whole church looked magnificent with the flower arrangements. After that, we went back to the house to get dressed for the celebrations. The bride looked like a doll with her beautiful lace dress, and her blonde curls falling gracefully down to her waist. At the church, we got all emotional seeing her walking down to the altar with Antoine, her proud father. Cecile's groom was not only very elegant and good-looking, but also uncomplicated and warm-hearted. I did not know these people at all, but they had been so welcoming and friendly to us. It felt like I was part of the family.

During the ceremony a young man came to sit beside me. He did not stop smiling at me. He was tall and slim, looking quite smart in his dark blue costume. He had a pale face with fine features, and his short frizzy dark hair revealed his mixed blood.

After the ceremony, we all went to the house of the groom's grandparents where the reception took place. When we arrived there, my eyes went wide. The garden was a large park with beautiful big trees with hanging roots. The driveway led us to a huge colonial house, with a veranda lit up with lanterns. On the lawn, a white gazebo had been installed for the buffet, and several cooks were standing behind their Primus stoves, adding the final touches to the food simmering in enormous pans. There was a smell of curry and of roasted beef, a huge number of grilled langoustines, and fish had been placed on beautifully decorated tables, with purple orchids and even small pink pineapples, which made a colourful contrast to the white tablecloth. The band was already playing traditional music, the Sega, creating a most joyful atmosphere.

The younger generation got together instantly and Catherine and I joined them. We were so excited to be in this wonderful place with these beautiful people that we ate very little of the good food. Everybody spoke in patois with us, taking it for granted that we would understand them and we did, but when we answered back in our own jargon, they all laughed. We were so happy, and like everybody else, we danced endlessly into the night. The young man who sat next to me at church had also joined our group. As soon as he saw me, he came towards me and introduced himself. He stayed at my side that whole evening. I felt I had met an old friend whom I had lost years ago. The next days he called me on the phone, speaking to me in an affected French accent, caused by his years of study in France.

Jack invited me to his place, a white house that he had shared with his sister Noelle since their parents bought a small hotel on the island of Praslin. An old man who, apparently, was once in the Foreign Legion, had found shelter at their place. He lived in a room of the house. This man was quite fascinating with his old wrinkled face and his vivid blue eyes. He soon was very friendly to me because I bought him cigarettes. We had a chat together and he spoke to me in creole with a strong English accent. On the day I left the Seychelles, I was quite moved to see that he had tears in his eyes when we said good-bye. I gave him a little photo of me as souvenir.

One day, together with our hosts, we flew to Praslin in a small airplane. Someone came to fetch us in a small rusted quad car and we drove along the coast. The roads were of battered earth, the nature still unspoiled; there were just a few houses hidden by incredible vegetation. We arrived at the little beach house belonging to our hosts, and at sunset we walked on the beach to collect heart-shaped cockles. We stayed at the water's edge, pressed the wet sand with our toes and where small holes appeared, we dug in the sand with bare hands to find the shellfish. When we had collected a full bucket, we went back to the house to find Marlene, our host, already busy in the kitchen. She washed the white small mussels thoroughly under the tap to get rid of the sand, and plunged them into a spicy bouillon. This was served with hot crispy bread. Our dinner that night was so frugal, but we ate like kings on the patio, sitting on simple rattan chairs. Marlene had picked some hibiscus flowers and placed them, one by one, stylishly on the white linen tablecloth. Only candles lit the place, enabling us to sit outside without attracting mosquitoes and other bugs.

After dinner we went to pay a visit to Jack's parents at their charming hotel on the island. Once more I was very warm-heartedly welcomed; Jack's mother had heard of me from her son. Time flew away so fast and we had to go back to our little bungalow. The following days, Jack and I spent as much time together as we could, and we went out every night with our friends. It was one of the best times of my life; I was really on a pink cloud.

Catherine was having a really good time as well, but I noticed that her behaviour towards me had changed. She was, as if on alert, snapping at me from time to time. One night I saw her kissing Louis, one of Marlene's sons. I reminded her that she was a married woman, and asked whether she was aware of the consequences of her behaviour. She was the wife of a colleague of mine, who was very ugly I must admit, but whom I liked very much. I was behaving quite well at my hosts' house and I was expecting the same from Catherine. But she said she was just there to have fun. She went on being very unfriendly towards me, and one day when I offered Louis money to pay for the fuel for his car, she said "oh, at last!" raising her arms in the air. She probably did so to give her lover a bad impression of me, having forgotten that I had paid for her flight to the Seychelles. I did not earn a lot and did not really have much money left. What a strange woman. She seemed to hate me now for some reason. She was dangerous.

Sadly our holidays came to an end. Jack had red eyes when he hugged me good-bye at the airport. I had to go back to my family and take on the role of Cinderella again. My parents came to the airport to fetch me. My father, true to himself, immediately made a speech about the explosive political situation at the Seychelles and how many innocents had been imprisoned since the putsch there some months ago. He always acted as if he knew everything better than anybody else. I was unable to express myself, to tell them about my stay there; nobody asked me if I had a good time.

Afterwards I started to write to Jack regularly; pages and pages about my everyday life. He also wrote to me and life seemed more tolerable whilst I waited for his next letter.

I started to visit Catherine after work, because I thought I could share my feelings for Jack with her. One day, when I went to her place, her husband – who used to be so friendly to me – did not join us at all. He stayed in the living room watching television while Catherine and I had diner. She did not give any explanation about his strange behaviour, and acted as usual. But when I went to say hello to him, he seemed to be angry and was very cold towards me. So I left and never went back there again. I was never invited either. It took me at least a year to find out that Catherine had lied about me, telling him that I had behaved like a slut during our stay at the Seychelles. I suppose it was her way to shield herself in case I divulged her love affair with Louis. She really did not know me; I would never have told her husband or anybody else. She had done me wrong; in the eyes of her husband I was a disgrace. He did not stop gossiping about me in the office, telling incredible lies. Even his mother, a very ordinary woman, spread stories about me, although I did not know her at all. This was ridiculous, because Catherine was continually having love affairs and everybody knew how she was. Her husband was the only one who seemed to be unaware of anything. Nobody at the office paid attention to his stories about me; they thought that he was a fool. But it caused me problems at work, because he was my subordinate. I had studied and passed the exams as an underwriter, and I had been promoted to work as the first female underwriter in the office. But suddenly Catherine's husband sent me to the back, away from the clients, to disappear behind mountains of renewal forms to be sent by post. I was no longer an underwriter, just an underwriting clerk. I was frustrated and bored. When I asked about the sudden change in my work, he told me that he was following orders from management. I knew he was the one behind it all. I stayed in that upsetting situation, unable to do anything; a victim of the system, working in a company belonging to white people. Everybody knew that a white person earned higher wages than a black individual, even if they were both doing the same job. Being a woman meant that I earned much less than a man too. There was no union or syndicate, nobody to protect you. The worst was that people of mixed race like Catherine's husband were always ready to sell their soul to the white as soon as they had been given a privilege of some kind. The creole was a dangerous man, because he was a hypocrite and envious. If any creole, intelligent and talented, reached a good position at his job, there was the danger that another creole would try to bring him down. The touristic brochures talked about a country where all races walked hand in hand; this was only a façade.

I went on living my life without showing my anger, hoping to find a way to get out of the unhappy situation. I longed to leave everything behind me. I could not afford to live on my own; my salary was ridiculously low. I had to find another job, something completely different. The fighter in me drove me to start learning German as a way to open new doors.

Chapter 11

———◆———

Two years passed since I met Jack, and although we kept writing to each other, I really did not know what to think of this relationship, which had stayed platonic the whole time. I decided to go, once more, to the Seychelles; this time alone. On the day of my arrival, Jack was also coming back from a trip to the United States where he had spent the holidays with some cousins. We met at the airport. I was excited to see him, but when he saw me he said abruptly: "Don't expect anything from me."

What an affront, a real slap in my face! What was this all about? I thought that he was in love with me; all those love letters he sent me, telling me how he missed me and wanted to see me. I was a proud person and was really offended by Jack's sudden change of mind. But then again, the little girl in me took it all in her stride like so many times before and acted as if she did not care. We went to his house and he wanted to have sex immediately. He was not the lover I expected him to be. I immediately regretted anticipating so much in a relationship with him. I was ready to give him love and had opened my heart to him, but there was no trace of passion from his side. I looked at him from a different angle, found somebody superficial and without any personality. I realised that he was too weak a character for me. I had imagined someone, and my imagination had drawn me far away from reality, from the real Jack.

Following my survival instinct, I paid attention to the nicer things surrounding me. I found a new good friend in his sister Noelle who was so beautiful and so nice. She spoke to me very openly, and warned me about her brother, whom she thought was not only immature but also very selfish. I met John again, the old legionnaire who was living in the house. While Jack and Noelle were at work, I spent hours with the old man. I took care of him a little, bought new curtains for his room, nice bed sheets and other accessories, which transformed his tiny living space into a real *'garçonnière'*. John was so proud of it that he invited all his friends, the seniors of the village, to his place, and they also became my friends. But Jack was not happy about my friendliness to the old man. He thought I was being too generous, and even showed his disapproval when I offered him a cup of tea. I was not wearing any rose coloured glasses while looking at Jack anymore; he was lazy and lacked ambition at his job. I was always paying for us both whenever we went out, and he started to criticise me.

One day we went to pay a visit to friends of his, whose son had been jailed for political reasons: He had been suspected of being against the new government. The Seychelles were in a state of repression at that time. The young man had finally been freed after several weeks of detention. He seemed to be quite traumatised, and his mother was telling all the visitors how he had changed and was scared to go out. While everybody was discussing the political situation, I saw Jack smiling at a very beautiful girl who was sitting in a corner of the living room. He could not get his eyes off her. I just knew that she would be the one to replace me as soon as I left his house. Years later, Jack told me that he had a very brief relationship with that girl just after I left.

Two days before my departure, Jack wanted to go dancing in a very chic hotel on the island. We got there, danced for a while, then Jack pointed at a man who was at the bar, and told me he had to say hello to him. I followed Jack without thinking, and saw a tall German with blue eyes. The man looked at me intensely while Jack was showing off, talking to him in German. The man's name was Karl, he was a lawyer in his mid-forties. There was a German woman standing next to him, she was obviously younger than him. She had beautiful, long, dark blonde hair, but her face was quite funny, out of proportion with high cheekbones, a large forehead and a narrow protruding chin. Her eyes were shifty; she seemed not to look at me. She was very slim and I knew that she was the type of woman who used her body to attract men. But Petra, that was her name, did not stay with us while we were talking to her friend. She went dancing all by herself on the dance floor. Soon enough, young locals surrounded her and she became exuberant. Karl invited us to dinner the next day. He started to talk to me, asking me about my country. He could not take his eyes off me for one second; dancing with me the most languorous slows while showering me with compliments. Jack was getting upset, and I suddenly became more important in his eyes. He had to show the German that I 'belonged' to him. He became more demonstrative towards me, kissing me tenderly and holding me by the waist. His sudden attention was faked; I ignored him and talked to the foreigner. This was too much for Jack, who decided to go back home. But Karl asked us to give him and his girlfriend a lift back to their hotel. Once there, Karl asked me for my address, expressing the wish to visit my country one day. While we were exchanging addresses at the reception desk, I saw Petra murmuring something in German to Jack. The next day Jack refused to go to dinner with Karl, saying that he was not interested in meeting the German guy again. It was obvious that he did not want me to meet this man.

On my last day at Jack's house, I said good-bye to John, the legionnaire; he cried, knowing quite well that he would never see me again. Jack's sister Noelle hugged me, and we promised to keep contact. At the airport I kissed Jack good-bye, but he seemed quite in a hurry to get away from me. At the gate I turned once more to wave him good-bye but he had turned his back and was already talking cheerfully to someone. I returned back home, knowing that my love story with Jack had come to an end.

Chapter 12

I went back to the office, looking for something positive to hold on to. I found friendship with those colleagues that shared my interest in culture. There were quite a number of intelligent young people. We read all the books that we could find and we discussed them intensely during our lunch breaks. A few times a week I went to a sports club to work out with some of my colleagues, or went jogging in the nearby sugarcane fields until the sun disappeared on the horizon. On Saturdays, I always visited an ashram to practice Hatha yoga with an adorable Hindu lady. I was leading a very healthy life, one could say a harmonious life, even though the atmosphere at home had not changed at all; in fact it was infernal. Jack did not write anymore. I was not sad about it, feeling rather angry with myself that I had thought he had a noble character and had fallen in love with him.

After some weeks I received a letter from Karl, the German. I was surprised, because I had completely forgotten about him. In his letter he talked about love at first sight, '*le coup de foudre*'; he had feelings for me. I really did not know what he was talking about. I just politely wrote him a few words back and Karl replied. This was the start of a long correspondence. I learned more about him; he was a renowned lawyer in Munich, freshly divorced and the father of two teenagers. Petra, the woman who accompanied him in the Seychelles, was his secretary and his mistress of five years, and his wife had left him because of this relationship. But Petra was repeatedly deceiving and betraying him. Their trip to the Seychelles had been a last attempt to save their relationship, but it had not worked.

On my birthday I received flowers from Karl; not a simple bunch, but at least twelve, which we placed in every room of the house. This was extremely funny because my brother became jealous and said that the house looked like a cemetery on All Saints day. Shirley, my sister-in-law, was completely flabbergasted; I had a lover. She was furious and dying of jealousy. She told her friends that I was making a mystery of my life and that I was a secretive creature. She was right, I never confided in her. She was not a friend.

After a year of regular correspondence and phone calls, I received a flight ticket to Germany from Karl. He wanted to see me and felt lonely. I asked my father what he thought about it, and to my astonishment, he told me to go. This helped me to take the decision of visiting Karl in Munich, taking two weeks leave from the office. Of course all my relatives were informed of my trip. Aunt Juliette and her daughter Josephine came and helped me to pack; everybody was talking at the same time. They were really excited for me and did not wish me ill. I showed them a photo of Karl and of his children. My mother suddenly told them: "This man seems to be very hard. She has met her master."

Until now she had not really expressed her feelings about the whole matter. In fact she had been quite friendly to me and in a relatively good mood since she heard about Karl's invitation. So when her comments came out of the blue, I was quite relieved. My mother was still the same; however, instead of slapping me in the face, she has chosen to hurt me with words. It was the confirmation that I had to take this opportunity to escape from my present life. But my mother, in all her insanity, was a very intuitive woman. I would one day find out how right she was about Karl.

Chapter 13

The flight to Germany was long. A nice lady sitting next to me in the airplane advised me to buy some tights at the airport. It was quite cool in Germany, she told me, and spring had just begun. I was freezing in my little pale blue suit while in transit at Frankfurt airport. Everything was so big and white, it was as if I was walking in a fridge, feeling quite lost, all alone, struggling to find the correct gate for the next flight to Munich. I was afraid and was having doubts about my decision to leave the island to go to a country with such a bad reputation. I did not know this man, Karl. But I was taking the risk because I really had to leave my home, go as far as I could, far away from this surrounding mediocrity, from this mad mother of mine, from this lack of love from both parents, from my brother and his devilish wife. One day they acted as if they liked me, the next day they rejected me and treated me badly. I had enough of their offensive words, of a sister-in-law who hated me just because I was in her territory. I had to go, to be myself. On the island this was not possible, I was kept in a cage, all these people suffocating me, wanting to take control of me since my childhood. They were my cancer, spiders slowly niggling my inner self. I had to be brave; I had been so brave until now. I had to fight now and build a new life, the life of my dreams.

I arrived in Munich; a policeman in a not very flattering green and beige uniform asked severely what I was doing in their country. I was afraid of the Germans, having had relatives of my father sent to- and killed in a concentration camp during the Second World War. Karl was at the airport; he was too cheerful to be natural. I sat next to him in his big Mercedes and he drove me to his house.

As soon as I got there, I met his sixteen years old son, Fabian. He was so embarrassed. I had never met somebody so inhibited before. He stood like an idiot, moving awkwardly from one leg to the other, holding his head down and answering in mumbles. I thought that he was mentally retarded. On the island even the simplest of the people were able to shake hands with you and talk to you. I could not understand how a European could be so strange. Fabian could not look into my eyes when I was talking to him.

The house was cold. The whole atmosphere was bizarre. I had a bitter taste in my mouth, a feeling that would come back again and again for the next fourteen years of my life. I was afraid of Karl like a pupil would be afraid of an old teacher. He was affectionate and, on the whole, patient. From time to time, however, he showed you that there was no choice; you had to follow his rules. He never had to raise his voice; he only spoke in a cold tone while his eyes turned a hard grey colour. I was so uneasy, knowing nothing at all of his habits, his tastes. I did not have a clue about German cuisine; the whole culture was so different from ours. He drank herbal tea without sugar at breakfast. I thought I was going to cry when I tasted this strange mixture; I was used to my mother's best English tea.

Karl had breakfast with his son very early in the morning. Fabian ate in a chaotic way; he reminded me of a dog. The boy was so skinny, and he hid his face behind a long fringe of hair. When he left the table, his trousers were full of breadcrumbs, which he did not even brush away. He had a deformed body, like an old man who had pulled a cart all his life. While he walked, his arms would hang alongside his body, they did not move. I thought the boy had a problem with the motor functions of his brain. He kept his head down and his speech was inaudible when he talked to his father. I decided to avoid watching this strange spectacle any more, and left father and son alone in the mornings. But Karl did not stop talking positively about his son; so intelligent, just a little lazy; if Fabian's behaviour was so strange this was only the fault of his mother. Anything that turned wrong in the family was his ex-wife's fault. She was to blame for everything.

I had my first encounter with German people when I went to shop in the village. I had to speak in English, because my German was very limited indeed. Nobody made the effort to understand me, because the Bavarians were not willing to speak in a different language. They were rude, aggressive and nasty. With my coloured skin they immediately thought I would steal. I was constantly being snubbed, or followed step by step in every corner of the shop. This was a hostile world, but I went into denial. I had decided that this would be the place where I would spend many years of my life, and I'd rather get used to it sooner than later.

I was good at housekeeping because I liked doing it. The house had an unpleasant, persistent smell that reappeared whenever we left it for a few days, but I placed flowers everywhere and gave the living room a feminine touch. But Karl planned my day, telling me what to do in the house. While Fabian was lying in the sun on a deck chair, his toes fanned out, I had to weed the garden because Karl had asked me to. I watched this son of his, and asked myself whether Karl was not looking for a housemaid when he asked me to come to his place. I found this whole situation humiliating; the son could be helping in the house too. His father spoiled the young man. Did Karl feel guilty for something? It was all very mysterious. Moreover I found it strange that somebody who claimed to be a multimillionaire did not have a housemaid in the house. My parents were surely not millionaires, but I was used to a higher standard of living. At our house we had a gardener and a housemaid and we had a certain *art de vivre*, which made Karl look like a peasant compared to my family.

Fabian refused to talk to me, even though he could understand French; he was learning the language at school. Every day I tried to have a conversation with him when he came back from school, and every day he would answer back, making only strange inaudible sounds. He left me to shut himself in his room until his dad's arrival. I began to take the train to Munich to explore the charming town by myself. When I came back home in the early evening, it was to see that the heavy curtains in the living room had been drawn together, and in the dark room there was that suffocating old man's smell that did not leave Fabian. He was always lying on the sofa, and on the coffee table there was a total mess of food and a mountain of newspapers. Fabian used to prepare his lunch himself, some pre-cooked food in cans that he ate in enormous quantities. He always ate on the sofa in the living room, and left the plates and cans and plastic bags all over the place. I had to open the windows and pick up everything while Fabian hastily went back to his bedroom, taking it for granted that I would tidy up after him. I very soon learned to hide some of the food I had bought earlier, before the boy could come downstairs and scoff everything he would find in the cupboards. One day he ate at least three kilos of fruits in half an hour and then I had to face a reproachful Karl, who thought I had not bothered to do any shopping at all for the family. His children were never at fault for anything; that's what I learned in the few weeks I spent in his house. Karl's son was chronically depressed; he had no friends, never laughed except hysterically sometimes, and the only music he listened to in his room was heavy metal. He wore the same clothes every day; some of them were torn but he did not care. He seemed to find comfort in food. But every time that I spoke about Fabian, his dad became upset with me. Karl was totally blind and only saw the genius in his son. I never saw the geniality of the boy, even years later. Karl thought that ignoring a problem would make it disappear. He refused to see the truth about his son.

The weekends were a complete disaster when Karl's daughter came to visit us. She decided from the very first moment to hate me. She was thirteen years old and obviously thought that she was cleverer than me because I could not speak German. She was determined to destroy my relationship with her dad, and every time she entered the house she tried to give me the worst time ever. She played the teacher, and made me repeat German words. I played the game even though it annoyed me. I wanted to tame this stupid, hysterical girl. But years later she told me she was convinced that I was totally simple minded! She was right; at that time I had completely lost my way, and I let them all treat me badly. How I regret not smacking her in her pink face at least once! It was very hard for me. I wanted to adapt as quickly as possible, but there were more and more obstacles on my way. I did not speak the language, I had no friends, only Karl, who told me that he loved me and needed me, but he was never there. He had no friends either; he had no time left for anything because he was working relentlessly.

Nevertheless I decided to hold on and to fight; I wanted to overcome these burdens. But the happiness I dreamt of was not to be seen anywhere. I did not think of happiness anymore, I was so anxious to adapt myself to this new life of being a perfect hausfrau, the perfect housekeeper.

When my overseas leave finished, I had to decide what I should do with my life; stay in Germany or go back to the island. Karl urged me to stay. He was absolutely sure of his feelings for me; he wanted to live with me.

The decision was only mine. It was much harder for me; if I stayed in Munich I would lose my job in my home country and even if it was not well remunerated, it was still a job. Losing it meant I would have to try hard to find another one if I decided to go back one day. I knew that I would be completely alone in a foreign country, and was going to become the stepmother of two volatile children. I was so young, only nine years older than Fabian, but the tougher part would be to deal with Karl's daughter who seemed determined to be very nasty to me. I had to learn the language as quickly as possible. But Karl promised the world; he would always be there for me. He promised that he would support me financially if ever we ended our relationship. I reminded myself how often I had longed to unchain myself from my family, so I took the decision to stay in Germany, knowing perfectly well that a difficult task was ahead.

Chapter 14

As soon as I called the manager of the office to tell him that I was not coming back to work, the news was like a bombshell. My nearest colleagues sent me their love and said that they were going to miss me, but wished me good luck in my new life. My parents, as usual, did not show any emotions. My mother said she was relieved that I had, at last, met someone. My father did not say a word, but apparently he would rather I left the country to live with a German than stay home and marry someone of whom he would disapprove. My brother, the big know-all, told everybody I was mad; this German was surely a drug dealer or a pimp. Even his friends were shocked and sure that the man was a creepy one who would exploit me. As usual I did not say a word when I heard about all the nonsense. At least I had reached my first goal: I had left my family!

I was delighted when Karl decided to spend a few days in Italy, in Tuscany, with his children during the whole month of August. Their cousin was joining us; the young girl was very nice and enjoyed talking to me in French. She kept warning me whenever Elizabeth planned to do something nasty to me. Elizabeth was calling her mother all the time to give detailed reports of everything her father and I were doing. When Karl bought me clothes or shoes, she took the receipts and read them to her mother. She even tore a nice dress of mine. She was always pulling faces at me at dinner. Her behaviour attracted the attention of a guest sitting next to me, an Italian lady who talked to me about it in the lavatory. She warned me of the years of misery that would be awaiting me if I stayed with this much too old man and his horrible children. But I was so young, so naive, I thought the girl would stop hating me one day, not realising that her mother was also playing a bad role. It was fourteen years later that I found out that the woman was manipulating her daughter against me, giving me a hard time even though I had nothing to do with her broken marriage and her divorce from Karl. Frustrated women find pleasure in harming people. What a waste of energy, but it is much easier to hurt and offend other people than to fight for one's own happiness.

But I was enjoying my first trip to Italy. The beauty of the Italian people, their elegance, their constant chatting, and their lively and joyous moods charmed me. I learned at last the meaning of the '*dolce vita*', and fell in love with the country. Even if the children were present, Karl and I could at last enjoy each other's company. We had four whole weeks to learn to know each other. The evenings were for us; we went out for a drink after dinner, leaving the children in their rooms, and did some shopping, as the shops were open until midnight. When we came back to the hotel, we often found Elizabeth lying in our bed. She was hoping her father would ask me to go and sleep in the children's room. But without a word and even before her father had noticed her, I gently woke her up and pulled her out of the bed. She always acted as if I was waking her from her deepest sleep, but her father carried her to her room.

Chapter 15

As soon as we were back in Germany, I decided to go to school to learn German. It was essential that I became fluent in the language in order to be independent again. I went every weekday to a private school in Munich. I met my friend Mathilde there. She was French, and lived in the town centre with her husband and their two small children. Mathilde took me under her wing, and thanks to her I started to have fun once again. This extraordinary woman had a bubbling energy; she just could not stay still. She knew every corner of the town, went regularly to the opera and visited the museums. She managed to become a member of the American Club through some connections, even though she could not speak a word of English. She painted huge and flowery motifs when she spent her summer holidays at the Cote D'Azur, and took part in local painting exhibitions. I followed her happily everywhere, very grateful and loyal to my intelligent new friend. She was the one who initiated me into the arts and classical music. Mathilde was the perfect loving mother, but she managed to keep some time for her own activities. That is why she was so happy. We spoke the same language, we had the same French culture and I could at last confide in somebody.

She gave me courage. Being older than I, she had acquired a certain wisdom and taught me how to keep distance from my problems and control my emotions; something that was quite difficult for me to do.

Mathilde hated the German language, and she never succeeded in mastering it. She was so French! She often waited for me at the entrance gate of the school to persuade me not to attend the course. We would run away like two naughty girls, giggling all the way to the café at the corner of the street. We spent hours in antique shops. My progress in learning the language was very slow, mainly because of Mathilde's influence. But it was as if God had sent to me a loving big sister to teach me how life could be fun. Mathilde was very refined and she was an artist in her soul. This prevented her from being arrogant like her compatriots. She was very open-minded and knew countless people in the city. At first some of her friends looked at me quite perplexed, asking themselves why Mathilde was so fond of me. But they became very friendly because I was discreet and reserved, and most of all, I was not eager to belong to their group of *bourgeoises*. I felt at ease in the company of some of these women, bohemians at heart, eccentric and with a real interest in the arts and music. They all lived in Munich because their husbands worked for big international companies in the city. They felt lost in the Bavarian world so they kept together in a microcosm, loved or hated each other, envied each other, sometimes copied their alter ego by buying the same car or the same furniture. It was really fascinating to hear all the gossip from Mathilde!

After six months I had to go back to the island to pick up some of my belongings. When I arrived, I was shocked to see that my mother's mental state had worsened. She was suffering from paranoia and thought that some nasty, envious colleagues were following her. She decided to retire well before her time because of that. She had started to have fears for her son, who she thought was in danger and surrounded by malicious people. Her suffering was real, but her sisters were without compassion and were really cruel towards her. Aunt Juliet did not hesitate to shut the door in my mother's face every time she went to visit. They all laughed at her incoherent stories. I was very sad for my mother; she was such an intelligent and elegant woman who used to be so appreciated and respected at the hospital. All this did not count anymore; from now on she was the clown to her relatives, who treated her without respect. Even Josephine's small children laughed at her and teased her, and it broke my heart to see that. But I was not really surprised that she had lost her mind; she had always been somewhat unstable. As a child, more than anybody else, I paid dearly for the consequences of her irrational behaviour. I remember the frequent slaps in my face she gave me for nothing. She did me wrong, accusing the innocent little girl I was of playing dirty games with my brother. She made me feel guilty for things that I had never done: "The neighbour saw you; he told me what you were doing with your brother. You little whore! You should be ashamed of yourself. Go to church and confess."

She would make me go to church and I would kneel in the confessional and start lying to the priest, telling him that I had stolen a few rupees from my grandma's purse even though I never did such a thing. I never told anybody about her accusations, keeping the secret like a heavy burden; I was too ashamed. Madness or not, I never understood why I was the one she accused of behaving in an evil way. Why did she not blame my brother, who was much older than I? Why was I the guilty one, the one tempting my brother? My mother's love for her son went beyond her insanity. Her behaviour towards me, her daughter, was irrational. She was obsessed by my femininity. I do not know where her dirty thoughts came from!

After some weeks on the island, I returned to Germany, thinking that there must be a good reason why fate took me away from my family. I felt guilty for my own feelings of relief that my mother's madness would not hamper me that much. But I felt for my dad. My dad's misery began when my mother started to hear voices in her head. My mother often spoke aggressively to herself in the middle of the night, waking him up. My dad finally found some relief when he gave her some calming drops, prescribed by a psychiatrist who had been working in the same hospital as my mother for years. But Dad never had the courage to have her taken to the psychiatric hospital, perhaps because she had herself worked there for so long, but more because he was ashamed of her insanity. He refused vehemently, even when my brother and his wife and all the others urged him to do so. My father secretly gave my mother these calming drops, pouring them in her tea in the morning. This medicine would calm her down, leaving her completely haggard. When she became too apathetic, my dad diminished the dose. He let her behave badly until he could not tolerate it anymore, and then added some more drops in her tea. But as I already said, my mother was very intuitive; even in her madness she would suddenly be very mistrustful and refuse any drink or food. Until his death, my father took care of his wife, sometimes he was absolutely desperate, sometimes absolutely angry at her but he never, ever, let her go. If only he was not so prejudiced and had found some real medical help and expertise. During the early years, I took her to Germany with me for three months. When she returned to the island, I was left completely drained, a total wreck, having had to deal with her madness and aggression. But after some years she refused to come to my place, telling me that it was so boring to be with me, even though I really took great care of her, granting her all her wishes and showering her with presents.

One day my aunts and cousins rallied together and ordered me to come back to the island to take care of my mother. She had behaved very badly at Juliet house. So they called me and told me that it was my duty to take care of my sick mother. But I knew that they were also very jealous of me, and that my mother's state of health was an opportunity for them to put an end to what they called my 'holidays in paradise'. I discussed the matter with my father who was completely opposed to it, telling me that my family was now in Germany. He said that my brother and his wife were there to help him.

Chapter 16

One day Karl went to Frankfurt to take part in an eso-teric workshop. At the beginning of our relationship, Karl led a fairly normal life; he drank alcohol, ate meat and had what I could call a normal sexual life. But when he came back from this first workshop he decided to change his ways of eating, becoming a vegetarian. He did not touch a drop of alcohol anymore. I had to learn how to cook vegetarian food and became, after some years, a specialist in all gratins! From time to time Karl ate fish. But Fabian and I took advantage of every visit to a restaurant to order the juiciest steaks ever. How I missed my father's cuisine!

Karl's personality changed rapidly as soon as he took part in esoteric workshops. He met these gurus, a lot of them charlatans who called themselves spiritual guides, whom he trusted entirely. I wanted to understand what was going on in Karl's mind and started to read all the books that he was buying. I do not know how I managed to follow him into his supposed search for spirituality during all these long years. I stayed true to myself never-theless, listening to all these theories, some of them absurd, without being drawn to them.

Karl started to follow healing courses; the laying of hands on the 'patient'. I followed the course as well, because I wanted to accompany him. The group of adepts consisted partly of desperate women in search of their soul mates. Karl was the only cock of the henhouse and all these women were just clinging to him, wanting him. Karl seemed to enjoy every moment of it, did not stop flirting and laughing loudly. He felt irresistible, and behaved like a stupid elderly gigolo. The women rubbed their bodies against his, touching him, purring like fat salacious cats. I was evidently the fifth wheel of the cart, disturbing them at their game. They were mad at me, jealous, envious of my fate; I was the one in his life, such a charismatic man!

I continued to accompany Karl to the courses but I could see how Karl was getting more and more on an egocentric track. Karl was a very talented solicitor, with a great deal of eloquence and presence, but it was obvious that he had an inferiority complex. To feel reassured, he had to be constantly admired. As soon as someone paid him compliments, he became joyful, beamed and straightened his bony, twisted back. He went to those spiritual sessions because the people who were there continually flattered his ego; most of them were very simple and had a lot of admiration for Karl as soon as he told them that he was a solicitor.

After some time he started a new course called: 'The Tao of love'. This put an end to normal sexuality. Karl had bought this book, which taught a sexual technique that enabled the man to attain 'illumination' or enlightenment. It taught how the man had to have sex but refrain from reaching orgasm, and using a special breathing method, transform the sexual energy into a divine energy. The adepts of this kind of teaching should pardon me, I am but a neophyte in the matter and I would never criticise anybody seeking spirituality, but all I know is that this teaching destroyed my sex life for the next fourteen years. I should have betrayed the old man and left him alone with his intolerable breathing exercises, but I was too stupid and stayed loyal to him. Karl used to call me 'my panther', but now the panther had to act as if it was dead in bed! Being a man, it happened that sometimes Karl could not 'retain' himself during intercourse. This made him furious; he stayed upset for the next three weeks, regretting his weakness. No enlightenment in view! Who was at fault? Of course it had to be me! I was the one, the obstacle in his divine path. He decided that we should sleep in different bedrooms.

Karl started to meditate in the mornings and evenings. I had to stay silent. In the evening, I was not allowed to watch television nor listen to music; nothing should disturb the man when he came back from work. I could never tell him anything about my day. This was of no interest to him. So I read for the whole evening and, from time to time, I watched him, exasperated to hear him inhaling and exhaling deeply and slowly. No music and dance in my life anymore, instead I had to hear the breathing of a crazy man. I would watch him and look at his ugliness; he seemed to be getting uglier and uglier while he concentrated in inhaling and exhaling. Karl seemed to be getting thinner, he thought that he was in great health but in reality he looked much older than he should. My God, why did I stay with this ageing dragon?

But Karl's excitement about the Tao philosophy disappeared suddenly, replaced by his next fixation; the Kriya Yoga. I went with him to a workshop in Stuttgart. We joined a group of people, young and old, a bit hippie-like. The atmosphere was quite pleasant and the teaching this time was not unknown to me. The guru, a fat and joyful Malabar seemed friendly to me. The women of the group were nice and I started to attend the course regularly. In fact it started one year after I had been living with Karl and I wanted to show him my willingness to share his passions. We met regularly at the house of the guru, generally for weekend workshops. We learned how to meditate, to breathe deeply while visualising the chakras, the energy points all along the spine. All this appealed to me until, again, the guru started to prohibit any sexual intercourse except for procreation. Again Karl took all this new teaching literally without asking me for my opinion. I was twenty-three and I was living like a nun. I started to look at boys, and there was a young man in the group who was really nice looking. Even though I flirted with him, I never went too far and stayed loyal to Karl. An elderly friend told me once that I was completely manipulated by him and that was why I never betrayed him. How I now regret not having had some fun with a man of my generation. I stayed with this aging, dodgy man and had nothing but tears in return. I sacrificed myself for him because I was so stupidly noble and I believed in him. I thought he was special.

The fat Malabar took his role as a guru very seriously. His face shone with satisfaction and he spoke in a gentle way. He had all sorts of anecdotes to tell, and apparently he was the grandnephew of a well-known yoga master. He was said to be the master's spiritual heir. The guru was just idolised by the members of the group. They all had plausible excuses for his small weaknesses; even the day that he tore a meniscus while simply trying to sit in the lotus position. This happened because he was so lazy, completely untrained and so ghastly fat.

The guru gave his lectures in English, and a skinny girl with a very beautiful and aristocratic face translated them simultaneously into German. Her name was Esther. She was quite strange; she never showed any sign of joyfulness. I felt that she had a secret; her behaviour was very mysterious indeed, but I liked her because she was intelligent. Esther belonged to one of the richest families in Germany; her parents were industrialists. A factory worker shot her father dead in front of her when she was still a child. Her mother took the reins of the firm very successfully, becoming one of the best managers of the country. But Esther did not get on well with her mother. As soon as the girl met her guru, she clung to him even though he was a married man and had a child. Esther called the fat man several times daily. Whenever she felt depressed, she asked him to come to see her at her flat and he would leave his family to go and see her. The man always granted her all her wishes, even if his wife was upset with him.

The Indian guru had financial problems. He asked the help of Karl, who lent him a huge amount of money, which was never paid back. But Karl was attached to this man. The Indian fox had seen Karl's greatest weakness, his ego. He knew how to manipulate him. The Malabar felt that I mistrusted him and started to 'work' on me. He gave me lots of advice, but I did not give a damn. He told me that my numerous talents were obstacles to my spiritual development. I listened to him without saying a word, asking myself to which talents was he referring? Did he think that I was too intuitive and might have seen his real self? Another time he told the whole assembly loudly and clearly how I had developed spiritually very quickly thanks to Karl, who was acting as my guardian angel, bringing me higher and higher every day, up towards the divine. He said that I had to be very grateful to him and to obey him. He added that Karl was my guru! These declarations made me laugh very loudly, thinking it was the joke of the year. But I saw how everybody was looking at me, quite shocked by my insolence. Most of all, Karl was very upset by my reaction. He did not stop reproaching me for my stubbornness; I was denying the fact that he was spiritually superior to me! He said that if the guru said so, I had to believe him. I replied that only God was my master and no one else; the Indian guy was not my guru, he could tell his tales to everybody else but me! But Karl let himself be too easily convinced of his special position before God. He thought he was invincible and would not listen to my warnings. I felt more and more estranged from the guru's world. Karl did not stop giving money to the man, because each time he was told that he had attained a higher level of spirituality. Moreover, I suspected the guru's particular attention to Esther was only because she was a very rich heiress.

Years after, I heard that Esther had had a child from the guru, who urged one of his nephews to marry her. The young man refused to be his uncle's alibi, and he returned to his home country, India, after a short time. The guru's wife finally filed for divorce. I was right not to have trusted this man who, while preaching for abstinence, was sleeping with one of his young followers and benefiting from her money. I was so upset with Karl who had totally changed his life and mine because of such a clown. Karl was shocked, but he stayed adamant that he was near to enlightenment and continued in his spiritual passion.

Chapter 17

After living with me for a year, Karl decided it was time to present me to his parents, who lived in Koblenz in an old-fashioned house near the Rhine. Karl's mother, Maria, was very strict. Once Karl entered the house, he was immediately drawn back to his childhood. I did not recognise the man anymore; he sat shyly on his chair and never contradicted his mother. His father, Joseph, fat and good-natured, was very ill and one could see that death was on his doorstep. He did not seem quite aware of what was going on around him, but he was in a very good mood. When he saw me for the first time, my caramel-coloured skin surprised him. He pointed his finger at me, and said: "Oh, she's totally black, I like her!"

So I gave him a big kiss on his wrinkled cheek, and he was delighted. This brought some lightness to the whole atmosphere.

Karl had an elderly brother, Gerald, who was the head of school and a maths teacher. He spoke in an authoritative way and corrected us for the silliest things. He seemed not to be able to forget his profession at all, and this made him quite ridiculous. But he was completely devoted to his old parents; he just wanted to be the good son. That upset his wife terribly. Eva was crabby, had cruel thin lips and was arrogant and nasty. At first sight, I knew she would hate me. For her, I was the foreigner from anywhere, brought cheaply to Germany to be her brother-in-law's new toy. In her eyes I was an illiterate, a stupid creature from the islands, and she made fun of me or spoke to me with condescension as soon as I opened my mouth. She never asked me about my occupation or that of my parents, I was just worthless, and she never changed her mind. But her reaction towards me was also the consequence of the hate she felt for Karl. Everything coming from him was completely rejected.

The house consisted of three apartments, each on a different floor. Gerald and his family lived on the ground floor. It was spacious, with views of the Rhine. Each visitor who entered the living room was struck by a huge painting of Eva's father, a former SS officer. There were piles of books and papers placed carelessly on IKEA shelves. This was the usual style adopted by many teachers, to enhance the impression that they were authentic intellectuals, caring neither for interior decoration nor for any other materialistic display. But for me, the lack of aesthetic care reflected disharmony in the family. Gerald had a strong feeling of duty towards his parents; he wanted to do everything perfectly for them. But Eva wanted him to detach himself from his blood family; she wanted him to be there only for her and their children. Her resentment towards her in-laws caused a palpable tension between them. Eva hated her mother-in-law and showed it openly. She was very ungrateful to this old lady, who loved her grandchildren and fed them even though she had also her own sick husband to care for. But Maria was also a very strong person and she ignored the nastiness of her daughter-in-law, continuing to do what pleased her while keeping an eye on everything in the household. At first I was really scared of the elderly woman, but slowly I began to like her. I must admit that this was made easy for me as I lived very far away from her and only saw her sporadically. But she was a very honest person and fair towards everybody. She spoke to me about Karl's divorce from his first wife; how she suffered from depression and could not take care of her household and her children. But she spoke also about Karl's untruthfulness and lack of devotion towards his wife and children, living only for himself and his work.

When, later, Maria came to visit us at our place, she knew that I had much to learn, but instead of criticising me, she taught me a lot in the kitchen and I was grateful to her for that.

All these people were stuck in their little prejudices. When Joseph, Karl's father, died, I was not allowed to attend to the funeral because I was not married to Karl. He went without me, and decided to spend some days with his mother to comfort her. Gerald and Eva had a visitor in their apartment at that time, a young married woman from Paraguay called Claudia. She was apparently very beautiful, and she chose to travel to Germany to find a substitute to her boring husband. Of course she flirted with Karl, and of course Karl could not reject such a beautiful woman. Apparently instead of mourning, Karl had a very romantic weekend. Eva was thrilled to witness their little game, and months later did not hesitate to give me a very detailed account of the whole story. She wanted to show me how unimportant I was in Karl's life. When Karl got back home, there was nothing unusual in his behaviour as he went back to working hard again. Some days later, I was cleaning his house like a good servant when the phone rang; somebody had a message for him. Claudia's messenger was apparently just an acquaintance of hers who was asked to let Karl know that she was coming to Munich in a few days to see him, and she wanted him to find a hotel for her. I told the man that I was Karl's partner, and he became aware of the embarrassing situation he had put himself into. Karl entered the room at that moment and I just gave him the receiver. The devil acted as if he was surprised and told the man that he would not be in Munich for the next days and would not be able to meet Claudia.

It was a very humiliating situation. I had a huge row with Karl, packed my luggage and decided to return to the island, but Karl refused to let me go and told me that he did not want to see the woman again; she was running after him. I was so lost, and instead of going back to my country, I stayed in the lion's cage.

All this happened while my mother, my brother and his wife were visiting. They witnessed the whole drama, the scenes I made with Karl, my tears. They saw my dismay. I was a young woman who lost all trust in the man with whom she was living. But my close relatives stayed true to themselves; they showed no compassion. Instead, they told me that it was my own fault. I travelled much too often without Karl, leaving him all by himself. I was shocked to hear that from them. It was true that I had been visiting Rome some days before, but I had organised the trip for them; my dear ones, who had repeatedly told me how they wished so hard to visit Italy at least once in their lifetime! I had saved hard to be able to offer them the flight tickets to Rome and the hotel. Karl did not even know that I paid everything for these ungrateful relatives of mine. Even in Rome they let me pay for everything. I shared a room with my crazy mother, and I had to endure my sister-in-law's bad mood every time we were having a guided tour of the city or stopped at a museum. She did not want to learn anything at all; she hated anything with a hint of culture. It was such a waste to have planned all of this. Shirley would have preferred to spend all of the money on shopping. I insisted that they accompany me to the guided city tours; I was adamant that it was important to bring some general knowledge into their heads. One evening, I caught my brother in flagranti taking money out of my safe (he knew the password) but he just said that he was just counting what was left. As usual I did not say a word, even though I was shocked by his perfidious behaviour.

Hearing how they reacted to Karl's infidelity, I knew that these people would never be on my side if anything happened to me. I felt very lonely. I was aware that I could never be really happy in Germany with Karl. But the strangest thing happened; by betraying me and making me jealous, Karl had made me feel attached to him, like a beaten dog feels attached to his master. I did not want to lose him.

Before flying back home, my brother took me aside and had a weird conversation with me, warning me that if I ever came back home, I would be the shame of the whole family. Everybody would be pointing their fingers at me, knowing that the man rejected me. He urged me to stay in Germany even if I had to live all alone in a room somewhere. I could count on him; he would come and pay me a visit from time to time!

Chapter 18

Karl's betrayal was the worst thing that could have happened to me in that particular period of my life. It spoiled everything. I thought I could start a new life, away from my parents and all those who prevented me from being myself. But after what this man did to me, I felt so vulnerable and did what I should never have done: I turned to my family again. I had lost all my confidence. I started to feel homesick. I missed my mother, despite her cruelty towards me. I missed the selfishness and the lies of my brother. I missed the sarcasm of my father. But my own family had only one thought: I had to stay with Karl. They did not want me back. When I left the country to stay with Karl, my brother called him a pimp and a drug dealer, but as soon as he entered Karl's house in Munich, he smelled the money. In my brother's head, I was the idiot who could spoil everything, but he needed me to achieve his new goal; get the German guy to share his money with him!

I had no choice but to dry my tears, hide my anger, ignore my pride and stay with Karl. Worst of all, in all my despair, I truly thought that I could make my family love me if I was generous enough to them.

Luckily, my dear friend Mathilde was there to remind me that I was young and should have fun. She was the only one who understood my fears, but we did not waste our time together talking endlessly. Mathilde dragged me to a dance course for adults, then again and again to the opera. We liked being surrounded by these big-boned German ladies wrapped in their colourful evening dresses like giant candies. On a sad November day, we took the train to Salzburg because Mathilde thought it was absolutely essential to show me this fantastic shop where they sold Easter eggs all year long. Mathilde was my only friend, and Karl was someone who did not make friends with anybody. The only people who surrounded Karl were ass-kissers. He had twenty-five solicitors who worked for him, and they all treated him as if he was God. He was, no doubt, a genius in his profession. When I went to the office they surrounded me, smiling at me and complimenting me. It was all so superficial, it was clear that none of them would be a real friend.

Karl never showed any interest in the arts at all. He never came with me to the opera, because he abhorred anything that took him away from his mundane world. As soon as he came home, he went to see his son Fabian and dragged him out of his room for a long walk in the forest. It did not matter if the weather was bad or not. He tried very hard to help his son, to force him out of his shell, have a normal conversation with him. But this was not an easy thing to do. Karl followed Fabian's progress at school. He was adamant that his son was extremely intelligent, even though his school results were not very convincing. At first I tried hard to have a friendly relationship with Fabian, but after some time I felt that his depression was pulling me down as well. For my own sake, I left him alone. This strange situation stayed unchanged until he left the house ten years later.

Karl worked a lot, sometimes fourteen hours a day. He returned home exhausted and very agitated. After his evening walk with his son, Karl sat in the living room to meditate for one or two hours. To avoid any noise that would make him angry, I spent the time reading. After some months at the school of German language, I started to read German books, with a dictionary on my knees. These long evenings of a monastic atmosphere contrasted sharply with my days spent in town with my eccentric friend Mathilde.

A year had passed and my visa was expiring. Karl decided to marry me. He wished to have a discreet wedding, without his children. He did not want to hurt them. Nor did he wish to have my family present on that day. Karl being divorced, a ceremony at church was not possible. This made me sad, because I was a devoted Catholic. But I was twenty-three, and getting married was still exciting for me. I started to look for a nice wedding dress, which had to be short but chic. After some unsuccessful tries I fell in love with an adorable white suit, which suited me perfectly. It was in an expensive shop in the Maximilianstrasse. As soon as Karl came back home I told him about it, giving a detailed description of it all. But Karl asked me which colour it was and I said, "White, of course!"

He jumped to the ceiling and shouted "Not white, no, not white!"

His reaction shocked me; he wanted no party for the wedding, and I was not even allowed to wear a wedding dress. This clearly showed his lack of enthusiasm for the whole affair. He did not have the slightest thought for my feelings. I was a young woman getting married for the first time in her life, but not once did he ask if I had a special wish for such an important day. It was all and only about him. He must have thought that it was privilege enough for me to marry such a great man. But again I was paralyzed, overwhelmed by the situation, by the behaviour of this strange individual. I thought I had to stay put, not say a word and do as he wanted. I should stop thinking and stop complaining. After all, what a silly thing it was, to be upset about not being able to wear a white wedding dress! And I kept the pain in my heart. I started to realise that I was only a beautiful accessory in the life of this old man, a servant for his ugly monstrous retarded son and a scapegoat for his volatile daughter. But I had no choice but to swallow my disappointment. I could not go back to my country.

The wedding was a quick procedure; there was nothing romantic. Karl told me the date of the marriage only two days before. I had my hair done and was very beautiful in a silk dress from Louis Feraud. Karl brought me a wedding bouquet, and he ordered a photograph at the town council. The two witnesses were the secretaries of the mayor, grey looking and stiff. Sometimes I turn the pages of the photo album, and feel again the uneasiness that grabbed me by the throat. I see an old man, looking upset about getting married again. Holding him by the arm is a beautiful young girl, all smiles. I wonder how I could still smile so easily; even years later that smile would stay the same, as if nothing could destroy the child in me.

But I forgot to mention a detail that years later would make me sweat blood; the marriage contract! Karl brought me to his attorney a few days before the marriage. He told me there was a document to sign, nothing really important, just a formality. So I signed a contract in which I agreed to renounce all my rights as a married woman. I signed because Karl promised me never to leave me in a precarious situation if ever we divorced. He told me I had to understand, he had been through a divorce already where he had lost so much money. He had to protect himself from financial ruin. He had asked for the presence of a translator at the attorney's office. He wanted to make sure I understood all the terms of the contract. The translator, a French lady, pinched me and whispered not to sign the contract. I smiled and told her that I was not afraid. The attorney seemed lost in his own thoughts, frowning. He really did not seem very proud of himself. But here I was, smiling my disappointment away. I wanted to vomit; I signed this document, wishing myself good luck.

After the wedding I sent photos to my family. They were very curious about the dress, and wanted to know all the details regarding the ceremony. I received some criticism about the coloured dress, a lot of questions, but no presents, not even a symbolic one.

The marriage did not change anything in our lives. Karl continued to work as hard as before, returned home late evenings, ate alone and went for walks in the dark with his son. Everything was perfectly planned. On Sundays we had lunch in a restaurant in the forest, in the vicinity of our house. But we had to footslog for at least an hour before reaching the restaurant. Karl did not mind if it was snowing or raining cats and dogs. At first I liked those walks very much, it was all new to me; I was discovering the beauty of the autumn, the colourful leaves of the chestnut trees. But then the walks became boring; year after year doing the same thing, following my husband and stepson who walked so quickly, like blond zombies with long skinny legs. The men ignored my presence completely, talking to each other in their guttural language. I followed them at a distance, looking around me, wishing to have a glimpse of an animal, at least have a beautiful creature to look at. Fourteen years living with a man who could do the same walk again and again, often floundering in the mud, to reach the darkest restaurant I have ever seen.

Chapter 19

In winter we spent some weeks in Switzerland in Karl's chalet. It was in the Valais and there I was happy to be among people who spoke French. I loved spending time all by myself in the little town of Sion. I bought books and books, and sat in a café just to hear the charming accent. Their accent was quite different from Mathilde's, who was a genuine Parisian.

Karl's daughter, Elizabeth, joined us for the ski holidays and she made sure to be horrible to me. Whatever I cooked she would pull a face at or refuse to eat. Everything I prepared was 'disgusting'. She broke my little radio, which was precious to me. She said she could not bear to hear French. There was not much room in the pocket-sized chalet, and when I practiced yoga in the living room she jumped over me, screaming like a hysterical person. I did not react at all; she wanted to provoke me and I wanted to show her that I was stronger. I learned to concentrate on my yoga exercises and let my mind keep away from her. But she may have thought that I was completely apathetic. I was very sad, aware of how I had changed since I started living with these strange people. Where had the happy young girl gone? I was once so full of enthusiasm regarding my future. Now that I was in company of these people, I was incapable of thinking properly; I was just like a slow tortoise, completely debilitated. I could not do anything except to try my best to be tolerated by them all.

Everybody skied, so I had to as well. I still remember the early mornings, my cold feet stuck in these heavy, hard ski shoes, shaking and wanting to cry, clinging desperately to the damned ski tows, to fall down ungraciously at the summit, legs apart like a cockroach. I could stand it as long as I was in company of a ski teacher; he was patient and made me do things that were appropriate for a beginner. But the whole procedure changed to a nightmare as soon as Karl came to fetch me. He forced me to come down the slope, even taking the black pistes, shouting at me. Apparently I was behaving as a three-year-old child; I was a young athletic woman, and I should not make such a fuss. With military discipline, he skied with me until sunset, and as I got tired, I fell more and more often. Sometimes it was snowing so much that you could barely see around you, but Karl ordered us all to continue skiing.

One day someone told me that he could not understand my dislike for skiing, because it was so much fun. At the summit, you could lie in the sun and drink hot chocolate with a shot, and then after descending some slopes you had lunch surrounded with joyful people. The most fun was of course the 'après-ski', drinking and dancing in the big tents or in the pubs at the stations. I told him that I never saw my husband relaxing at the summit; we were allowed to have lunch but then we had to ski until late afternoon, the word 'après-ski' did not exist in his vocabulary! Karl was a masochist at sport and at work. Everything he did had to be extremely strenuous. If not, he said that it was a waste of time. He expected his family to do the same. How I missed the indolence of the islanders and their 'joie de vivre'!

The second winter we went to Davos, again a most dusty ski station in Switzerland. The people there were really unfriendly; we went to the same café for years and not once did the owner greet us. But during this second winter, I learned to practice cross-country skiing and I really liked it. The region was very beautiful, and you could ski endlessly on the tracks along valleys and rivers. What pleased me most was that I could stop whenever I wanted, without being afraid that a racing idiot would dash behind me. As soon as I was good enough, I went by myself, escaping from my annoying stepchildren and their authoritative father. I could at least indulge myself into some hours of peace before being terrorised again by Karl's daughter.

Years later I was spending the New Year's Eve festivities in a hotel in Arosa, Switzerland, together with the family and my nine-months-old baby. Cross-country skiing by myself, I was following a track in the vicinity of the hotel. Someone had told me to take a hidden track. At the start there was nothing special about it. The first contact with the cold was always painful, my legs were stiff and, as usual, my fingers were aching. There was no one but me; everybody else preferred to ski on the sunny slopes of the mountain. I continued to follow the track and could hear my skis grating the snow. I came out suddenly into a vast flat area, behind which were dark pine trees. At this same moment, the sun cut its sword through the fog and the sky became blue. An extraordinary light blinded me and there, all over the white snowfield, were crystals as large as my hand, glittering in every colour. I did a few slides very slowly, in real exultation to be in a place of such beauty. My God, how extraordinary! I forgot the cold and my aching feet and fingers, it was as if my soul had left my body to find itself in a pure heavenly place. If I found myself in such a beautiful place after death, surely it would all be worth it. At dinner, I told Karl about this strange and lovely experience, but he pulled me back to earth. He said that the warm smoke coming from the thermal station nearby caused the formation of the crystals. I did not care what he said, and kept the beauty in my heart.

Winter had its charms; sitting by the fire was so romantic and Christmas time was so very special with all the tradition and customs. I started decorating the house, inspired by the shop windows in town. I wanted to buy the best Christmas presents for everybody, not only for my family but also for Karl's children. Elizabeth never showed any enthusiasm at the choice of my presents, but Fabian was not very complicated and seemed pleasantly surprised. Karl's mother, Maria, sent us a big box full of self-made cinnamon and ginger biscuits, coated almonds and peanuts every year. She added a small present for each of us, beautifully packed with a little card attached to it. She really was a wonderful woman.

Chapter 20

Some time before our marriage, Karl bought a house on the island. To avoid complicated formalities, he bought it under my name. The house was built on an elevation, facing the sea, and stone steps led to the beach. The view was absolutely breathtaking. We took our meals al fresco under the large patio. I loved to sit there for breakfast, when multicoloured birds came to pick up the breadcrumbs. The garden was long and narrow with three enormous flamboyants, and big breadfruit tree. There were small mango trees and pomegranates, all of them covered with fruits during the summer. We had a watchman who was also in charge of the garden; he lived with his family in a little house at the entrance gate. His wife Lucie was a great cook, but she was very difficult to deal with. Marco, her husband, worked at the village bank as a messenger during the day, and in the afternoon he took care of the garden. They had small children who used to play on the beach. In the afternoons, after school, they used to spend hours in the sea, their strict mother watching them.

My brother found the house. He took a tremendous amount of time before he showed it to us. That was the drama queen in him, who could not resist making the whole procedure a theatrical event. First he dragged Karl and me to different places on the island; we wasted whole days viewing all kinds of houses, all of them worthless and unattractive. Karl was exasperated because he disliked travelling by car in the heat. When he finally said that he would like to stay at the hotel for the rest of his holidays, to find some rest, my brother insisted on showing us a final property. He told me he had kept this house for the end, to impress Karl and have him buy it before our departure to Germany. Karl was very upset with my brother's manipulative actions, especially because he had wasted his precious holidays driving around the island for nothing. But we liked the house very much. It was not very big, but had a certain charm with its yellow shutters and its French windows. We had a view of the small islands on the horizon. In front of us, the barrier reef protruded unevenly out of the sea, black rocks beaten by the waves.

At last, my first dream had come true: a house by the sea! I took years trying to renovate the house, giving it my personal touch, bringing some new accessories from Germany, but my brother always inhibited me. He had to have the last word on everything because he was the one dealing with the workers when I had left. I needed his help, and he knew it. He had really bad taste, and I had to struggle endlessly to have changes made as I wished. I remember wanting to get rid of an old bed and buy a new one for the guests. He told me he had repaired it to perfection. When I saw the bed, I was horrified because my dear brother had simply bought a large piece of plywood and placed it under the mattress.

One could see it sticking out of the bed. It was so ugly and I did not know what to say. Louis had no notion of decoration at all, but he was so confident that he expected me to be very grateful to him. Of course he told my mother and all his friends how essential he was to me. If I ever expressed myself and told him that this was not the way I wanted things to be done, he was very offended indeed and everybody, especially my mother, would pity him and be very upset with me.

Louis's wife Shirley started to take an interest in the house as well. This made the situation even worse. She was very tacky, and always bought the cheapest kitchen utensils and other accessories for the house. Everything would break after a very short time. For years and years I would go to my house, feeling excited and happy to see it, and after the holidays I would leave with a heavy heart, nervous and frustrated from fighting pointlessly for my rights. I had the feeling that the house did not really belong to me, because my brother and his wife were taking over. I was angry with myself, because I was still shutting my mouth to avoid fights.

Karl and I never had a moment for ourselves in that house. Too often my brother would come with his family to pay us a visit. He usually brought with him some of his friends that I barely knew. The visitors would come at any time of the day, especially on the weekends. No one ever called beforehand; they would come without warning. I developed the habit of staying in the garden, reading in the shade, on alert, expecting visitors any moment. Staying outside was the only way for me to prevent them from honking the horn of their car and shouting my name. I knew how mad Karl was at them when they disturbed him while he was resting after lunch. Karl usually spoke briefly to the visitors, and went swimming for hours while the guests drank whisky or beer, waiting to be entertained. Karl also loved to go for long walks on the beach. I would always accompany him. We walked for miles along the coast until sunset when we returned in a taxi or a bus. My brother and my mother also came with us. My mother was great at walking, going at a steady pace for hours, surprisingly calm. Sometimes some friendly dogs followed us, others menacingly showed us their teeth but calmed down as soon as we spoke gently to them. On our way we met some fishermen, simple and open-hearted, repairing their nets on the beach. There were also tourists, and whenever we met some Germans, I would flee from them discreetly, not wanting to hear their language nor converse with them. They asked too many questions and were always surprised at the sight of the exotic couple we were, Karl and I. There was a sort of skepticism in their eyes as soon as we started feeding their curiosity.

Very often, we went to one of the expensive hotels, to enjoy dinner in a nice atmosphere. We would barely mention going out, and my sister-in-law and my niece would get out of their lethargy and start preparing themselves for the big night. Karl was mad about their behaviour. He told me that Shirley's only interest in her life was to go out and have fun at else's expense. She did not use her brain for anything else, rejecting any intellectual stimulation. Her daughter was exactly the same. These two always stuck together, like twins. Shirley did not have any table manners at all; she ate with her elbow on the table, spoke with her mouth full and moved her knife around wildly when she was talking. Her daughter ate in the same dreadful way, and my father was absolutely appalled by it. But if he made any comment to his grand-daughter, she would just look at her mother and roll her eyes. My brother, who had received a strict educa-tion, did not seem to bother at all. He was very upset if anybody expressed his disapproval at my niece's lack of manners. It was annoying to see mother and daughter leaving the table as soon as they had finished eating, leaving us deliberately so they could wander about on the hotel premises as if they did not belong to our group. We were only good enough to pay for them.

I always returned to Germany with a strange feeling of uneasiness. We had been acting as if we were having a good time together, but there had been so many things unsaid, too many concessions on my part, just to avoid any conflict. My brother and his wife had been bowing to my husband because he was so generous to them. They were even sometimes very friendly to me, as if seeing me from a different angle. But I was not a fool; I felt Shirley's hidden hostility, heard her inadvertent neg-ative comments about me, and was aware of my broth-er's hypocrisy and exaggerated enthusiasm about Karl. One of these days I would have to pay dearly for my brother's good will. I knew that he had big plans. But I thought I had no choice; this family was the only one I had. I wanted to be part of it, even though I was quite aware that my sister-in-law had taken a more important place than I held in my parents' hearts. I wiped out of my mind all the thoughts and the premonitions. I tried to forget how I heard my sister-in-law and my niece saying such unpleasant things about Karl and me one night. They were lying together in bed, and we had just returned from an expensive dinner. I was too young and not strong enough to confront them. I could not deal with the loneliness that was awaiting me in a foreign country, with an equally strange husband, always busy and unavailable, insisting that I function by his military rules.

Chapter 21

After living together for two years, Karl and I wanted a child. But after a few tries, I still could not get pregnant. I confided in my mother; a big mistake. She asked me every week on the phone if I was pregnant. Her tone was accusative. Then she went on and on with her usual litanies: "It must be your fault. Your husband has two children from his first marriage. It can only be you."

At night I cried in silence, taking the whole responsibility on my shoulders. I repeated my mother's words to Karl, who said he shared my mother's opinion; the problem must come from me. After a year, I decided to go to a gynaecologist. A long and exhausting phase of my life began; I felt as if I had become a laboratory animal. I had to endure a lot of tests and blood analysis. I swallowed tons of hormones, which caused my breasts to grow, attracting men like bees to honey. But nothing helped. I was sterile, and I felt bad because Karl had started to act as accusingly as my mother. She told me, of course that God was punishing me because I was a bad person. I could never understand why I was a bad person in my mother's eyes. She just told me that I was bad, but could never say why. I think I was bad because I was born alive, even though she tried to abort me when she was pregnant. After another year of being a lab hamster, I went to find a new gynaecologist. Mathilde, my dear guardian angel, advised me to see a doctor who had the reputation of being infallible. I remember entering the doctor's surgery; how insecure I was. He was a tall man with broad shoulders and had brisk manners. He spoke loudly, and asked me all sorts of questions about my previous treatments. Then he looked at me and asked about my husband. As soon as he knew how old Karl was, he told me that he had to get examined by a urologist. Surprised, I told him that Karl had two children already. The doctor said that the children were over twenty years old. He said good-bye without giving me any more explanations, and while I was leaving his room, he told me in an authoritative way that I should not bear the burden of this matter by myself. Five minutes spent with this man, and all the guilt disappeared.

I had to convince Karl to go to an urologist. He seemed surprised by that request, and took his time before going to a doctor. I went with him when the urologist called him back for the results of the tests. Discreet, I decided to stay in the waiting room, but it seemed to me that the doctor kept Karl in his office for ages. When Karl came out of the doctor's office his face was livid. He held me in his arms. The doctor's diagnosis was really disastrous for Karl. He could not have children anymore. The man was totally infertile; this could have happened years ago, when he suffered from an infection of the prostate.

My first reaction was to feel very relieved. My gynaecologist was right; I was not the one at fault. At least now

Karl and my mother would stop pointing their fingers at me. But I did not say a word to Karl, and we went home. Karl thought he was so perfect, so invincible, so near to God, nearer than anybody else on the planet. Now he had to learn that this was not the case. I had spent years with that feeling of guilt; I had felt ill, and I thought that I was not normal. But suddenly all that was over. Karl never said he was sorry for his attitude towards me. But I was nice to him and did not refer to it, trying to be supportive. I wanted him to know that I was there for him.

But already Karl must have hated me, because I was the one who showed him, indirectly, that he was a human being with imperfections, like everybody else. If only I had known what his real feelings were, I would have left him and gone to live in France or the United Kingdom, starting another life all by myself. But how could I have imagined the thoughts going on in his brain, that he had such a big ego? I thought all I could do was to be loyal to him, my husband. After all, I married him for the good times and the bad times. But for Karl, I was the one who had thrown him off his throne. He had lost his invincible power in our couple. I was the one with a young, healthy body. He could not bear it.

After that Karl became obsessed by his infertility. He contacted all kinds of doctors, looking for a miracle treatment. He even told me that he wanted to ask his son Fabian for a sperm donation! I refused vehemently, shocked by Karl's sick mind. I sincerely wanted a child, but I still had both feet on the ground. A little voice told me that this was God's will. He wanted to prevent me from having a child with the genes of this strange man.

My gynaecologist offered me new possibilities as soon as he was informed of my husband's infertility. He talked about sperm donation and that he could find the right person for us. Karl agreed. I made an appointment with my doctor for the artificial insemination. Everything went very fast, luckily for me because this was a rather unpleasant procedure. I got pregnant at the second try. During the whole pregnancy I had a very harmonious relationship with the doctor, and Karl was ridiculously jealous of him. He was sure that the donor was nobody else but the doctor himself!

Following the latter's advice, I waited for the third month of pregnancy before telling my family. Unfortunately for me, my parents came to visit me with their granddaughter. What a stressful time! My dad never stopped criticising Karl, he went on and on with his comments. Then he started to criticise the German food, not edible! Even the beautiful expensive fruits that I bought were tasteless, not like those he ate in Australia. My father was in bad mood because he did not eat his meat and drink his whisky like he used to. But it was summer, and we went to Switzerland to a nice hotel. There, again, the food was not good enough, moreover he was always arguing with Elizabeth, Karl's daughter. These two hated each other. All day long Karl, true to himself, dragged us all on those long tiresome walks, and in the evenings I had to take care of my niece, who was still small at that time. Her grandparents had wished to take her with them, but they were incapable of taking care of her. They lay down to rest before dinner and expected the small girl to do the same. Nobody asked me if I was tired or not. When he returned to the island, my father told everybody that my husband was an idiot without culture, who had forced him to walk stony paths for hours. He had not once been invited to go to the opera, not even to a circus! We never invited him again to our house.

As soon as they were gone I found real peace of mind. My pregnancy was going very well, and I was practicing yoga for pregnant women. I was watching my weight carefully, ate healthy food and not for two; putting on just twelve kilos by the end of my pregnancy. I found all those dresses for pregnant women so unattractive. So I bought normal dresses, just two sizes bigger. Karl made an effort, and seemed to be caring for me. I had forgotten the trials of getting pregnant and I was happy, waiting with excitement for my baby to come. I was as active as an ant, and decided to make big changes in the house before the birth. We transformed the basement into a real paradise for my stepson Fabian. He was given his own apartment with French windows, an en-suite bathroom and a small terrace. I wanted more space on the first floor, transforming Fabian's bedroom into a new room for the baby and me. But Fabian did not want to lose his bedroom; he was against any change in his life. I stayed resolute and did not change my plans because we had only one bathroom upstairs and Fabian liked to spend hours in the bathtub. I waited for him too many a time and saying nothing, but with a baby, I was not willing to be that tolerant any longer. Apparently he complained about it to his mother and sister. They pictured him as a male version of Cinderella, the poor victim of his stepmother, sent to live in the cellar! His grandmother, Maria, came to my rescue, saying that it was a privilege for a boy of twenty-one to live in such a beautiful apartment. Nobody talked about it again but Fabian, influenced by his sister and mother, did not pardon me for what I did to him.

Time was passing, and I was getting stronger mentally. I used to call my mother once a week, listening to her nonsense and usually felt bad afterwards. One day she announced, using again this usual tone of hers that drove me mad: "The child will be called Raphael and I will be his godmother!"

I snapped at her that the child was mine, and she was not to decide anything about him. I hung up and decided that it would be better not to have any contact with her until the birth of my child. It was so important for me to live the last weeks of my pregnancy in peace. I listened to classical music more often than normally. I continued to meet my girl friend Mathilde to have a good laugh, joining her in her numerous wanderings. My old neighbours were very nice to me, impatient to see the baby, really touching, sending me small gifts and good wishes. This was a period of my life in which I was really happy. My pregnancy was a privilege, a gift from God, and I was grateful for that.

I gave birth on a stormy winter day. The doctor praised me for my calmness, which impressed Karl very much because he always treated me as if I was an unstable person. My baby was a nice-looking boy who had a striking resemblance to my father. The first person to be informed of the baby's coming was my friend Mathilde. She was also the very first person who came to see us at the hospital. She came and took photos of my baby and me. What a joy; Mathilde was like a sister to me and she was so delighted to see my beautiful baby boy.

The atmosphere was quite different at the visit of Karl's children. They were embarrassed, maybe because their father was acting even more strangely in front of them. He felt guilty once again. Their visit was very short because their father pulled them away from the baby's cot. He decided to take them for a walk around the hospital. They did not show any joy to see the baby; they just had a look at it without a word. I told myself to be extremely careful with them, because I feared they might do something to harm my baby.

My room at the hospital was so full of flowers that I could not keep them for too long because they smelled too strongly. The flowers came from Karl's lawyers and clients. We received so many presents and congratulatory cards. My brother and my sister-in-law sent their good wishes, as well as my aunts and cousins. My parents were surely happy to have a grandson, but I did not hear from them at all. My mother, who devoted herself totally to her granddaughter at her birth, did not offer to come and help me with my baby. I thought this was for the best, even though it was quite hard to return home by myself after some days at the hospital. Karl did not even take time off to pick us up at the hospital; as usual he gave priority to his work. His chauffeur came and brought us to our house. What a warm welcome from a father to his newborn son!

Paul was the name I chose for my son. At first I felt uneasy whilst taking care of him, scared to do something wrong, totally untrained. But I soon got used to being a mother. Everything went smoothly. Soon my little boy started to smile at me tenderly. Being a mother fulfilled my life completely. I felt real love for the first time in my life. Nothing bothered me anymore; the lack of love I had experienced before, the hate in the eyes of some people, all the pain caused by my mother during my childhood; all this belonged to the past. I was able to give all my love to this precious little creature, and for the first time in my life I could do it without fear of being hurt. My son gave me all that love back.

Chapter 22

When Paul was five months old, we decided to go to the island for his grandparents to meet him. But as soon as they saw him they showed their disappointment because the baby did not look like his father, Karl. Of course, I never told them about Karl's infertility and the in vitro fertilisation I had undergone. They could not understand how the baby had brown eyes and an apricot-coloured skin. They would have preferred him to have blue eyes and blonde hair. His pink cheeks and his nice features did not alter their disappointment at all. Pulling a face, they inspected the baby from head to toe while saying how sad they were that he looked so much like me. Paul, who was a very good baby, started to cry. Some time later, under my brother's convincing arguments, I made the mistake of leaving him with my parents just for two hours. When I came back, Paul was wailing. My father told me that I should give him some medication to soothe him, he had not stopped crying since I left. They were all saying how nervous he was, just like his mother. They were already starting to interfere in the way I should bring up my child. This made me determined to keep Paul as far away from my family as possible.

It was traditional to pay a visit to all your relatives when you were back in the country. But these numerous visits really were tiresome for me, because I was breast-feeding. I had to present myself at my best, well dressed, with my hair beautifully done, as slim as before. There was such pressure. Having shown the baby to my aunts and cousins, I returned to the house by the sea feeling weaker and weaker after driving for hours. I was the shadow of myself, I lost a lot of weight and I was losing my hair. Instead of comforting me, Karl told me that I looked old! This was typical of him; he was upset to see me getting stressed by the whole situation. For him there was nothing difficult in what I was doing. I was making a fuss. But he was having a good time, doing nothing, just relaxing at the beach, refusing from the start to accompany me.

Believe me or not, I continued to pay a visit to my aunts for the next ten years of my life. The pressure stayed the same; I never stopped dreading their criticism.

To please my parents, I decided to baptise Paul on the island during our stay. The ceremony took place in a small church surrounded by sugar cane fields, near our house. I asked a colleague of mine to be Paul's god-mother. I liked her because she was such a creative person. For the baptism she filled the living room with white flowers and decorated the table with a white damask tablecloth, silver cutlery, crystal glasses and the best china that I brought from Germany. My baby had a beautiful white outfit and I put on a white dress also. It was as if I was unconsciously celebrating my wedding as well. It was great, and even better when Lucy, our fantastic cook, started to serve the meal. My dad was our photographer of the day, and even my mother seemed very pleased. But I had offended all my aunts and cousins by not inviting them for the celebration. This was because my brother and sister-in-law did not wish to see them in my house. When I went to see the old women and brought them some cake, they asked me if this colleague of mine was better than them; maybe I was ashamed of them. I was sad and embarrassed because I could not tell them that I had followed my brother's instructions. The more I thought about it, the more I felt angry with myself. I had done something that I did not want to do: I had planned to invite everybody on that day, but again I let my brother and his wife take over and have control over me. I did not confide in Karl about all this. I did not want him to be aware of all the conflicts and intrigues in the family. They all smiled at him and were pleasant to him; he could not know the intricacies in the family, how jealous and envious these people were. There was not much love in paradise.

After all these agitated weeks we returned to Germany, where my only occupation was to take care of my little boy. This made me so happy; I was made to be a mother. Nothing else really mattered. I knew that Karl had changed and was more distant from me. But I did not try to do anything about it; in fact I got used to his cold-ness. He was even more distant to his two big children, and this displeased me. I felt responsible for them as well and I tried my best to improve the situation. I gave Fabian as much warmth and support as I could, even if it was a euphemism to say that his response was not very convincing; the boy was as indifferent as a dead fish. Elizabeth was quite the same, continuing to be nasty to me but I thought that if I kept being nice to her, it would finally calm her down and she would surrender. After all we were a family.

My son, Paul, was quite small compared to the German children of his age. When Eva, Karl's sister-in-law saw him, she said that he had rickets. That was, of course, not the case. But I think that Paul was small because his father forced us to be vegetarians. Under his heavy long fringe, Paul observed the world; he had a very good memory. When he was one year old, he fell into a fountain in Munich and, instead of being traumatised, he developed a passion for fountains. In the summer we used to go frequently to town, and during our errands we had to stop at every fountain. Paul was still being pushed in his buggy but he would tell me where to go like an authentic city guide. We watched the movement of each fountain, counted the seconds before the water splashed out again. He ran around the fountain, laughing, happy to play with the water, getting completely soaked most of the time.

As he reached the age of three, I started to travel with him to the most beautiful cities of Europe. We visited museums, and he seemed to like art as much as I did. From London to Barcelona, from Vienna to Berlin, we saw so many different and marvelous works of art. We spent more time at the Natural Museum in London or the museum of Egyptology in Berlin because these were museums with more subjects of interest for a child. In Venice we preferred to spend time at the Guggenheim museum rather than the Academia; there the visits were kept short to avoid boredom. Paul was a very happy little boy, very open to the world. Perfectly bilingual, he felt at ease everywhere he went. He loved his father, adapting himself to his lifestyle. He accompanied him and his half-brother Fabian during their walks. But all went wrong as soon as his father forced him to ski for hours. It was Karl's military education that made the little boy hate sports in general.

He really liked to spend his summer holidays at our chalet, in the Valais in Switzerland. We walked along the 'bisses', irrigation trenches dug all along the side of the mountains, some of them dating back to the fourteenth century. We would take the gondola at Anzere, a ski station and a ghost town in the summer, and walk all the way down to the Rousses, stopping at a refuge called 'La Cabane des Audannes' which was set in a stony and strange landscape, at an altitude of two thousand and five hundred metres above sea level. Our Dalmatian, Amour, was a strong member of the group. He kept walking behind us, which was quite unusual, but he was quite aware of the danger; the paths were narrow and the precipice very deep. We acquired the dog when Paul was four years old. Eva, my German sister-in-law could not believe her eyes when she saw the dog. "How come?" she said, "Are you getting on in your family so well that you even bought a dog?"

This woman seemed surprised that we seemed happy. But I just wiped her out of my mind; Amour was a member of our family and we could not imagine our lives without him.

Chapter 23

Even though I was a happy mother, I still wanted contact with my family, calling my mother regularly. At the end of the phone call, I always felt hurt by something my mother had said to me. But the following week, I called my tormentor again with a joyous tone and told her about my little boy.

My other relatives were no better, they took me for a milk cow. As soon as I called them, they told me that they 'absolutely' needed this and that. I was always sending them packages filled with shoes, or a hat for a cousin who was invited to a wedding, dresses and lipsticks. But I could never satisfy them. The lipstick was not the proper colour, and the shoes were not as beautiful as they thought. Sometimes I was told to buy something for a friend of a cousin, someone I did not even know. I was spending a lot of money for all these people, having to give up my own personal wishes and needs. Karl was not very generous and I was doing all this without his knowing. I was never thanked for all the presents. They all took my good will and generosity for granted. It was as if it was my duty to do so.

My father offended me quite often if ever I called on Sundays at the wrong moment. I would hear his angry voice in the background barking to whoever had answered the phone: "Tell her that she is disturbing, nobody wants to hear from her now." So I would say good-bye, feeling rejected by my family. No, they did not miss me at all.

I was only a child when I had to deal with my brother's lies. He loved to tell stories made up to impress the others. My mother was the only one to believe him unconditionally. Louis had a tendency towards megalomania. In his stories he gave himself an important role. I never took interest in what he was saying, and tolerated this weakness of his. Later on, as an adult, he continued to lie, manipulating everybody around him to achieve his goals. It was surprising to see that his wife lied as much as he did, but in a concealed way.

My brother managed to trick me while I was in a phase in my life when I was determined to win the love and respect of my family. I was stupid enough to think that if I were good to them and generous, they would, at last, accept me as one of theirs. I was so obsessed by this idea that I completely forgot how wicked they were. My brother must have sensed it all. He started calling me, which was very unusual. He even told me how much he missed me. He never stopped talking about his daughter, how sick she was, always suffering from hay fever. It was so humid and rainy where they lived. From one telephone call to the other, he just complained about his daughter's bad health and how worried he was. He thought she had asthma; she was probably allergic to the pine trees surrounding their house. Then one day he told me that my niece's doctor had advised them to leave their home and move to a drier region. He was looking for houses on sale on the coast but they were unaffordable. He did not know what to do; he even went to pray at the grotto of Saint Ignace, he was so desperate. He started crying.

I was such an idiot, imagining Saint Ignace's warm hand on my shoulder, his loving eyes looking at me, giving me his approval. Without asking Karl first, I just told my brother: "But the gardener's cottage is going to be free very soon. Why don't you renovate it and go and live there?"

What a wonderful sister I was, absolutely fantastic! How generous! No one has ever been so good to him! Thank you! Thank you! Thank you! I am sure that he was thinking how clever he was, and how manipulative!

The gardener's cottage was at the entrance gate of my property. This house was quite old and small, but it had blue shutters and the patio was beautifully decorated with blue ceramic flowerpots. There was a huge tamarind tree near the house, and enormous green ferns were growing all around the tree. A wall made of dark volcanic stones separated the house from the rest of the garden and gave privacy to the family living there. I loved the house and the vegetation around. I thought, in my naiveté, that my brother would keep the whole as it was, just modernizing the kitchen and the bathroom.

My brother took care of all the formalities, but avoided showing the real plans to me. What saved me in this dodgy episode was that Louis wanted to reduce the costs and he built the house without changing the plot of land into his name. Officially the house was mine. My brother used a document that allowed him to use my bank account to pay any bills for my own house. So he used the same document to sign whatever he needed for the construction of the house. He had the liberty to do as he liked, because Karl and I travelled to the island only every two years.

So two years later when we arrived at our house I was totally flabbergasted by what I saw. Just in front of our house stood a huge residence of colonial style with huge columns. The gardener's cottage had been demolished, and with it the wall that separated it from the rest of our garden. The huge tamarind tree had been felled to let a huge terrace invade our territory. Nothing, really nothing had been done as I told him to do. My brother took twice as much land as was previously agreed. Our garden was badly damaged, all dry and bare. Some grass was growing miserably where the pomegranates used to be. Lucie, the cook, told me that my brother had a huge hole dug in my garden where they buried all the concrete and iron sheets and everything from the demolished house. When I reproached him about what he did, he asked insolently if I would have preferred to have the lot in front of my entrance door.

Karl and I were also appalled to see that a couple of Germans were living in his new house. My brother was renting the house to a hotel director and his ugly wife, a real grey mouse, who immediately gave us the impression that we were the intruders. Well prepared for any question from Karl and me, my brother told us that he had to rent the house in order to pay for the mortgage he had taken from the bank. He added that he had hoped for more financial support from my part but that I never offered him anything. He never mentioned the health of his daughter anymore. She was showing no sign of asthma or any other illness.

After the shock, I called the gardener and we tried to save my garden as well as I could. My whole joy of having a house by the sea had completely disappeared. I went back to the house for some more years, but I never felt at home anymore. My brother had taken from me the only material thing that belonged to me. I was having a hard time in a foreign country, and I always thought that despite a disadvantageous contract of marriage I had something of value from my husband. But now with my brother and his house on my own grounds I had been deprived of my only financial security.

During our stay at the house, we constantly had to face this German woman, who was so depressed. She had to walk beside our house to go to the beach, always with some other women of her nationality. Their children were spoiled and kept running everywhere screaming and shouting. One day we watched one of the mothers beat her child with a huge stick. When I called out loud from my window, she threw the stick in the middle of the garden; leaving it there without respect for us. The gardener bought a new motorcycle and he gave the women driving lessons on our driveway. They drove back and forth from the entrance gate to our own doorstep, not thinking of the noise they were making. Karl put an end to their game by having a serious talk to the gardener. The German woman hated to live on the island, and she hated its inhabitants. She was always trying to have a talk with me, but it was all complaints, criticising even the school system on the island. Her children went to an international school, and she was telling me how the level of education on the island was much lower than that in Germany. I told her that the high school certificate or baccalaureate certificate was internationally recognised. I mentioned that the majority of the teachers working in the international school were Europeans, so maybe they were at fault; it might be wiser to send her children to a public school. She seemed quite annoyed by my advice. Lucie, the house-maid, worked at the Germans' house in the morning, and when we were there, she came to work for us in the afternoon. But the German woman would send her two children with her, and they stayed at our place and annoyed us all, jumping on our beds, breaking our china and making a lot of noise. After one of the children hurt himself in our house and the mother complained the next day that I had not cared for him, I told Lucie that these children were not to enter my house again. The grumpy woman liked the company of Lucie who, despite her qualities as a cook and housemaid, was completely illiterate. This friendship surprised me, but I understood that the woman was having problems in her marriage, and Lucie was the only person in whom she could confide. Her husband, the hotel manager, was betraying her with a Chinese girl and was having a really good time on the island. Contrary to his wife, he told me that he could live there forever. But at the end of his work contract, he was sent back to Frankfurt where the couple divorced. Lucie went to visit her friend and was disappointed to see that she was still moaning about her life even though she was back to civilisation!

The problem with my brother's tenants continued. Another married couple came to live in his house. This time both husband and wife were French. My brother told me that they were so friendly, much nicer than the Germans. I thought them to be even more intrusive, with their excessive familiarity. I noticed that the gardener was taking much more care of the garden near their house, neglecting our side totally, even though I was the one who was paying him. Naïve as I was, I never controlled the money spent for the house, taking it for granted that my brother was spending my money accurately. I gradually had a strange feeling that there was something wrong with my brother's explanations whenever I asked him about the expenses of the house. But I refused to see the truth. I felt that, at least materially, I was secure with my husband; he would always be at my side to take care of me. Why should I bother about my brother cheating a little bit with my money? But I was wrong not to be cautious; my brother was getting bad habits, thinking that my money was his. I had given him too much control over me. I was losing ground; even my house did not seem to belong to me anymore. I felt more and more like a stranger to that place.

Chapter 24

When Paul was seven years old, I sent him to an international school, because I wanted him to learn English just like me. Thanks to Paul's new school, I made the acquaintance of women of different nationalities. I soon made friends with them, and I started to have a very interesting social life, while at home my stepson Fabian was becoming more and more strange. He had finished high school and was starting to study maths and statistics at the university of Munich. His father was, of course, very proud of him and told everybody how well his son was getting on with his life. But I had already noticed that Fabian was in his room too often, lying in his bed or taking a shower for hours. The poor boy was not getting on well at all. Staying for hours in hot water was a way for him to seek some warmth. He never had the love of his mother because she was chronically depressed. His father still just refused to see his son's illness, even though he repeated that he loved him. As for me, I was no better. I never succeeded in taming the young man and making him feel better, even though I tried really hard to show him my affection. Fabian was jealous of Paul, his half-brother. He refused to play with him, and seemed irritated by the child's presence. So the small boy soon reacted like everybody else; he avoided his big brother and was even a little afraid of him. When, at last, I understood that Fabian had stopped attending his courses at university, I informed Karl about it. As usual, he reacted too radically. Karl sent his son to a building contractor who made him work as a labourer. I knew that this was not going to solve the problem, because the boy was not going to cope. But Karl refused to listen to me; my opinion did not interest him at all.

After some months, Fabian disappeared. He left the house without a word, taking with him luggage and a credit card. He left us in anguish, and his father felt terribly guilty again. Strangely, as soon as Fabian was gone, another sort of atmosphere could be felt in the house; lightness, a feeling of new life. We were no more surrounded by the dark and opaque aura of a chronically depressed person. Even though I sincerely worried for Fabian, there was another part of me that felt relieved; I could breathe at last, but of course I did not say a word about it to Karl, I did not want to offend him. After a brief time, Karl began to work as frantically as before. He kept silent at home and never spoke about Fabian. Whenever he talked to me, he did it with a new coldness; his tone was harsher. I felt that he thought I was responsible for the disappearance of his son. He regretted that I came into their lives twelve years ago. Elizabeth, my stepdaughter, took the opportunity to tell us how miserable her brother had been at our place, a real martyr. I did not react to these accusations; I shut my mouth, as usual. Elizabeth ignored the fact that her brother was totally rejected by their mother. She even refused to invite him to her place, even for a weekend. "*Das ist fur mich zu belastend.*" (This is too much of a burden to me,) she once told my husband, when he asked her to spend some holidays with her brother.

Karl was getting more and more bitter; he even kept his distance from Paul, whose energy and good mood seemed to annoy him. I felt embarrassed to laugh in my husband's presence. Karl had put an invisible wall around himself, and looked at me without love whenever I talked to him. Again, this was his way of rejecting any failure in his life. Such a disaster should not have happened to him, it was not in his life plan. To consult a psychiatrist would have been the confirmation of his son's illness. Karl could not accept having a son with a mental disorder. For years, I had to hear that his first wife, Fabian's mother, was the one at fault. She was the cause of Fabian's depression. The woman was a bad mother, depressed, untidy, and lazy; she never did anything for her son or for the household. Now it seemed to be me at fault; my bad character had caused his son to leave his home. But Karl forgot that there were only a few years of difference between Fabian's age and mine. I could not replace his mother. On the other hand, Fabian, following his father's ways, had always felt superior to me, making fun of me, talking ironically to me, as if I was the idiot in the family; but this was a way of hiding his ill-being. His depression was very difficult to bear; I had to protect myself from his negativity. Slowly but surely, his unresponsiveness to my friendliness resulted in my talking to him only if it was necessary. I always took care of his clothes and tidied his room, however, always making sure that he left the house looking neat and tidy. Months before he left the house, he had an untamed beard hiding his skinny and pale face, but when I mentioned it to his father, he acted as if he did not notice the change at all.

After two years, one of Karl's colleagues finally found Fabian, thanks to a friend in the police. Fabian was living in Dortmund. Keen to undertake anything to help Karl, I told him that I would go there and find his son. I took the train with Paul for a trip, which lasted six hours. We stopped in Düsseldorf, booked a room in a hotel there and the next day we went to this rather grey town called Dortmund. I took a taxi at the station, and gave the driver the address that I had written on a piece of paper. I could not believe my eyes when the taxi stopped in front of a derelict building on which a pink sign was flashing, it said: 'Sex Shop'. There seemed to be some flats on the first floor of this weird place but I did not know where my stepson was, and there were no names on the main door. I let my little boy wait at the door and entered the sex shop, which was surprisingly quite busy at that early time of the day. All the men there stared at me. I went straight to the cashier who, thank God, was the owner of the whole building. Very German, he did not hide his annoyance at my questions but I insisted, and he finally called an unkempt woman and I followed her up some dark stairs. She told me that it was just a room that Fabian was renting, and opened a door. I was appalled by what I saw; grey walls surrounding ten square metres of dirt, a small bed against the wall, and a table with an electric ring on it. My heart broke to see the pigsty where my stepson was living. There were bags of trash under a little washbasin that smelled of urine; Fabian was probably using it as a loo. The bed sheets were colourless with dirt; all this reflected the disastrous state of mind of my stepson. I gave the woman two hundred Deutsch Marks and asked her to tidy up the room and wash the bed sheets. She promised to do it. I begged her to give Fabian my address at the hotel, telling him to contact me. I left the place with a heavy heart and Paul and I took the train back to Dusseldorf.

Fabian came to see me at the hotel while we were having breakfast. I invited him to eat with us and he rushed to the buffet. He had lost a lot of weight. He was wearing an old pullover, and the bones of his shoulders showed through it. When he finished eating glutton-ously, I spoke to him and he told me that he wanted to live alone. I told him to come back with me, just to see his father who had been so desperate; he could return to Dortmund whenever he wanted to. I promised to make sure that he received some money from his father to help him live a more decent life. Fabian hesitated, then said that he would come with us. We took the next train to Munich.

I called Karl from the hotel, and he was waiting for us at home. He wanted to talk to his son privately, and the next day Fabian returned to Dortmund without saying good-bye to his half-brother or me. I asked his dad to make sure that he had a little money for his food and other necessities. I brought Fabian back to his father but I did not know that very soon, father and son would make a pact against me.

Chapter 25

The next summer I went on holiday to the island with Karl and Paul. My mother fainted while we were sitting together having a little snack at the newly built waterfront in the capital city. My brother took her to the hospital immediately and the next day she had to undergo a serious heart operation. I spent my whole holidays taking a taxi every morning from the hotel where we were staying and driving for two hours or more to get to the hospital. Paul came with me, but I left Karl by himself at the hotel most of the time. This was a constant dilemma for me, because whenever I told the other members of my family that I had to stay, at least every two days, at the hotel with Karl, I had to listen to their criticism, saying that it was natural for a daughter to stay at her mother's side when she was so ill. They were upset that Karl never came to visit her. But Karl did not want to, and he did not care that I was never at his side, he was so busy flirting with the other hotel female guests and staring at their bare breasts. One day, feeling very uneasy about my husband, I stayed at the hotel and told him that I would like to go with him to the yoga session. He refused vehemently. I saw him, later, in the shade of some coconut trees, sitting in the lotus position, chatting and laughing with an open mouth with two blonde women. I had to go back to hospital the next day because my brother and a cousin had called me, reproaching me for relaxing at the beach in a luxurious resort while my mother was dying.

On the same evening, I had an argument with Karl because he was staring at every single young woman, smiling at them, even though nobody seemed to be interested in the old man he was. He just ignored me all the time, even though I was all dressed up, looking very pretty and young. His behaviour was getting less and less bearable and I told him so, asking him what was going on in his mind and if he had any feelings for me anymore. I added that if he did not love me, he should say so. But he did not reply, looking at me with coldness. I did not know that he was already cheating on me.

It was the end of August when we returned home and Karl rushed to his office, staying there until late, apparently having meetings. He told me one night that he had been to a bar with his colleagues for a drink. I found that very strange because he never drank alcohol and he never socialised with anybody. Soon the quarrels started. He snapped at me, criticising me for everything I did or said, telling me to shut up. Paul told me one day, in the car, that he could not listen to our fights anymore. His words opened my eyes; suddenly I became aware of living in an atmosphere full of tension. Karl never made a tenderly gesture towards me anymore. One evening I went to see Karl in his bedroom wanting to make peace with him. I hugged him and told him that we should be more loving to each other. But he pushed me so brutally that my head hit the wall and he screamed: "Your eyes are so full of hate. Go away, I cannot stand your dark energy, your aggressiveness anymore."

I was shocked; my husband scared me.

After some weeks Karl asked me to go to Dortmund to visit his son Fabian and persuade him to spend Christmas at our place. My husband had this strange look on his face; this happened every time he was lying to me. I sensed the deceitfulness, but again, I was scared of refusing him anything. So I made the trip to Dortmund, even though I thought that it was quite unnecessary, as father and son were continually in contact on the phone. In Dortmund, after Paul and I had met Fabian, I tried, over and over again, to call my husband, but he was not in the office. Fabian travelled back home with us. I was sitting next to a young African, a football player in a relatively renowned German club, and we were having a chat about the difficulties of living in a country full of racists and nasty people. Feeling confident enough, the young man asked me, in French, about the strange-looking Fabian, and I told him most discreetly who he was and how I was taking him back home. The African looked at me and said: "Let's hope that you are not bringing a snake in your home".

He did not know how right he was.

Karl was waiting for us at the train station. He had shaved his beard and looked so white. When I asked him why, he replied: "I have nothing to hide anymore."

I found his answer very enigmatic. I did not know that my husband had had a mistress for some months. He had probably started his affair before we went on holiday to my home country, because his strange behaviour and his nastiness towards me had really started while we were in that luxurious holiday resort. Everybody was so envious of me on the island, unaware of how sad I was. I should have sensed that he was betraying me; I should have seen the signals he was sending me unconsciously. I had even seen a long blonde hair on the car seat and wondered whose hair it was.

As soon as Fabian stayed at our place, he started spying on me, listening to my telephone conversations with my brother. I was complaining about the nastiness of my husband towards me, and I was even speaking in creole so that my stepson would not understand me. But I did not know that Fabian was waiting for his father, late in the evenings, to give him an account of everything I had said to my brother and to my friend, Mathilde. Whenever I went down to the living room and joined them, they stopped talking and Fabian hastily went back to his room.

For Christmas, we all went to Davos, to the grimy hotel where we used to go. Karl had taken a room for himself, and one night he came to my bed for extraordinarily boring intercourse. No tenderness, not a word, but then suddenly I heard him saying a name, and it was not mine. I suppose he was missing his mistress and he slept with me imagining that he was making love with her. He left like an animal, without a word. This was so humiliating. I felt depressed and soiled. The next day I caught a horrible cold and had to stay in my room.

I told Paul that I had a fever and would not come down for dinner. Karl did not bother to come and see me. I cannot describe the coldness of this man and how dreadful these days were for me.

On Christmas day, he did not have any present for me, saying that he had left mine at home. Paul saved the situation by being happy with the presents that I had bought for him. We were all separated the whole day; Paul was skiing with me, while Fabian clung to his father. All of a sudden, father and son were the best friends ever. After those two weeks spent in Switzerland, we came back home and I was surprised to see that Fabian was not eager to go back to his hole in Dortmund. I asked him when he was leaving and he answered: "I cannot say, we have not decided yet."

What a mysterious answer; the 'we' was quite telling, but again I did not sense that the two men were plotting against me.

Then came the thirteenth of January, a Friday! I had been working every Friday at Paul's school as a volunteer in the library. It was fun to be among people who were nice and friendly. I came home with Paul after school, and was surprised to see that the dog was not there, neither was Fabian. I thought Karl might have come home early and taken his son and the dog for a walk. I can still remember how I was taking Fabian's underclothes, freshly washed and ironed, to his room, when I heard Paul rush down the stairs. He had a letter in his hand and was looking at me with a most horrified look; he said to me: "Mum, Dad left us."

PART TWO

Chapter 1

Paul found the note that his dad had left on his bed, or rather on the bed frame, the mattress having been removed. His departure had been carefully planned. My husband took all his belongings with the help of my stepson; that son of a bitch who I had helped to get out of the life of a tramp. On a piece of paper, ripped from one of his famously cheap notebooks, my deceitful husband has written these words in his ridiculously tiny and torn handwriting:

I am leaving and will never come back. I thank you for many things, especially for our son Paul, a great spirit in a little body. Respect him, like the Virgin Mary respected her son, Jesus.

Karl

This man had the guts to speak of Jesus and of the Virgin Mary. He put himself on the same level as God, while deliberately sowing despair and fear in my life and that of my little boy. I cannot describe the shock it caused us. I found myself kneeling on the floor, Paul holding me, in tears. I called all my friends and my brother to understand the whole situation. I took my son by the hand and rushed to take the train to Munich. I had a key to my husband's office and we went to see him, but there was nobody there. I had a closer look at his writing table and turned the pages of his calendar. He had rubbed everything off, but I could read the blank prints left by his pencil. I read the word, Davos. He was in Davos then, in Switzerland, with his son Fabian. I called his hotel and I was told that the whole office, the solicitors and the secretaries were there, even Elizabeth, my stepdaughter. He had invited them all in Davos to celebrate his birthday. So Paul and I went back home, totally devastated.

Some days later I heard from my homeopath, that my husband had sent a young woman to him because she had a cold. I did not know, then, that he had the nerve to send his mistress to my personal doctor. I suppose that the bitch was sick, too excited, having broken a marriage and of gotten hold of the very big boss himself.

When Karl returned back to Munich, he rented a flat in a village not far away from our house. He denied the presence of any woman in his life.

"No," he told me, "there is no other woman. I cannot live with you any longer because I cannot bear your negative energy anymore. You are going to make me sick. It is your aggressiveness. Even Fabian could not stand your energy, this is why he left us years ago."

Poor, poor Fabian, I suppose he had much better energy, surrounded by his trash bins and his washbasin full of urine. When I think of all I did to fetch him back home to his father.

Karl said that he would come back, maybe, he needed time to think: "I need to be alone, by myself, to meditate."

But it was all a solicitor's trick; he had already made up his mind to leave me and never come back. He was just lying to me to avoid a scene. What a coward, to leave his home like a thief and to give me all the guilt instead of telling me that he was shagging a bitch and was having fun. He knew what he was doing these past months, provoking me, arguing with me without reason. He did it just so I would answer back and he could tell everybody how aggressive I was. I was only trying to defend myself all that time. How stupid I was. This was the calculated behaviour of lawyers when they want to get rid of their wives.

Karl had the guts to come home every morning after he had left us, to have breakfast in our house. I thought he might still want to keep contact with his son and me. I let him in, instead of throwing him out of the house. I do not like thinking how I humiliated myself, begging him to come back, still not knowing that there was a woman in his life. Then one morning I went through his things and saw, in his wallet, a little yellow piece of paper on which was written: "I baked the cake for you. I hope you will eat it while thinking of me. I will kiss you wherever you want. Jacqueline".

Holding the piece of crap in my hand, I went to see Karl and asked him what the hell was going on. He did not know what to say; he just left the room, escaping from me. I ran after him, tried to prevent him from leaving because I wanted him to tell me the truth. I held him, pulled him back into the house. He grabbed me by my hair; I grabbed his other arm and bit his thumb so that he would let go. He rushed outside screaming "She is trying to murder me".

Poor Paul saw the entire scene. Years later he would tell me how his dad had reacted like a hysterical coward. But Karl had related the incident differently to everybody else, saying how I tried to murder him on that day.

I called his office and spoke to one of his lawyers. This one, I knew, liked me very much. He told me the truth: this woman was really Karl's mistress. She started working for them in July. Karl's secretary told me that this woman, aged twenty-nine, used to seek help, going to my husband's office in tears because she had problems with her landlord. She went to see him every day; soon the tears turned into moans of lust. This woman was living with a young mechanic, but she never hid her ambition for getting an old millionaire under her claws for big money. At work, she was known for her strong smell of sweat and the jogging trousers that she wore all the time. Obviously that must have attracted my husband, because after fourteen years of marriage I had become too elegant, too perfumed and too glamorous for him. Most of all, I had lost all admiration for him, tired of hearing him boasting about his intelligence and his high spirituality. I did not join him anymore in his exaltation when finding a new guru, whom he described as a mystic. I had brought him down from his pedestal because I knew all his weaknesses. Now he had found somebody else to flatter his gigantic ego. But for how long would she play his game?

Now that I had discovered the presence of this other woman in his life, my husband did not talk about returning back to me anymore. This was obvious.

Marley, an Australian girlfriend warned me: "Take whatever you can now; at first the husband feels guilty and is more willing to share; later he changes his mind and believes that he is giving far too much."

Following her advice, I asked Karl to give me the house, in which I intended to stay because it was important for our son, Paul, to be in his own environment. Karl said yes and booked an appointment with the attorney. But the day before the appointment, I was very surprised to see him paying us a visit. He was so nice to me, tenderly bringing me to my bathroom and begging me to have sex with him. I was curious to know why this man was behaving like an animal, so I did what he wanted, watching him. He thought I was his prey, underestimating me as usual. When he had finished, I could not help but notice how old and skinny his body was. It was disgusting, really disgusting. I wanted to vomit, but I kept quiet; an inner voice was telling me to be very cautious. He had the guts to tell me that now that we were tender to each other again, there was no need to go to the attorney and have the house put legally under my name. I answered as tenderly as I could, that now that the appointment was already made, there was no cancelling it. I said "Let's go and have the whole procedure behind us."

I saw him hesitating, not knowing what to do. Luckily he let go, embarrassed by his own hypocrisy. The next day we went to the attorney and I got out of the office, relieved that I had at least succeeded in getting a roof over Paul and my heads. I do not know how many times I thanked God and Marley for her good advice. Soon enough, I noticed how Karl was having regrets about losing his own house; he was attached to it like an old cat. His hate for me was increasing day after day. It was obvious that the woman had a bad influence on him. From a sordid background and very ambitious, Jacqueline knew how to please the aging man and make him feel young again. I was told how she accompanied him to his numerous spiritual seminaries. She was also a very good masseuse. Her skillful hands were even spoiling Fabian! When I think how this autistic individual had avoided any physical contact before!

It really hurt me to see my stepchildren's reaction to our broken marriage. Daughter and son were delighted that their father had left me, too happy to see me all alone with my son now. I thought I had always been good to them. I endured their impoliteness and their moody personalities without ever shouting at them. I showered them with presents, and gave them the attention that their father was unable to give them. I was not perfect, but I had done the best I could to those two ungrateful creatures. Only now, fourteen years later, am I aware of how much they had loathed my presence in their lives.

Most of all, I worried about Paul. The child thought it was all his fault, so I kept telling him that his dad had left us to revive his sexual life with a younger woman. I asked Karl to see his son regularly, but Paul refused to go anywhere with him unless I went too. He told his father that he did not want to see him without me, and he never wanted to see his half-brother again. Fabian was a traitor in Paul's eyes. Karl asked me to accompany Paul, every Friday, to a restaurant for dinner. On one of those evenings, we saw my stepdaughter, Elizabeth, sitting in her father's car. She sat proudly in the front seat and demonstrated how happy she was to send me to the back of the car. She wanted to join us for dinner. I knew she was leading up to something nasty. In the restaurant, for the first time ever, I had to listen to her making compliments to her father. Oh! How much younger he looked now! The separation really did him good!

"Sorry", she told me, "but I have to say that, because it's the truth!"

She kept caressing her father's cheek and kissing him from time to time. Never before did I see any sign of tenderness between father and daughter. While she was doing so, she would look at me, her white face showed her triumphant expression. I knew that I did not look good, I had lost two stone and I felt exhausted. But I did not show my despair, I acted as if it did not bother me; I spoke as if nothing had changed. I glanced at Paul from time to time and I knew that he had noticed his half-sister's game. As soon as Karl drove us back home, Paul kissed his father good-bye and, ignoring his half-sister, he said with a very firm tone for a little boy of nine years: "Papa, I do not want to see either Elizabeth or Fabian anymore. They are too glad that you have left my mother. Please tell your daughter that she looked like a whore, caressing you and kissing you like that."

That night my little boy decided to protect me. But I felt sad because I was aware that Paul had suddenly lost his childhood. He was anxious, sad, watching me all the time, asking me continually if I felt depressed. It upset me; in fact I found it unbearable to hear my son asking me how I was feeling. So I decided to take the situation into my hands and told him that he and I were now a new family, together with Amour, the dog. Papa had decided to leave us, but we would always stay together. I told him that we were now free to have a normal life, a better life, full of fun and joy. We would do a lot of things together, without asking for his dad's approval. We could listen to loud music at any time of the day. We could watch television in the living room, just like his school friends; we did not have to stay in the basement anymore to do so. We could invite our friends over and have parties at home. He gave me a big smile and said: "We can eat meat at home at last!"

I found this declaration so funny that I had a fit of laughter and we suddenly started jumping all over the place, the dog joining us in the excitement. From that day onwards, we felt better, not alone anymore. We were looking forward to a new life, feeling free.

Chapter 2

We started to re-organise our lives, little by little. I felt free to do as I wanted! I had to call my real self back to life. I was able to live a normal life and be more sociable. I told all my friends that they could call at our place at any time of the evening. But I had to be watchful too, because my husband had turned into my enemy. I heard how he was lying about me, telling people how aggressive and nasty I could be, how scared he was of me. The term 'mad' was the new word he was using to describe me. If I were really mad, would that have been a reason to leave me? Some secretaries from his office turned their back on me when they saw me in town. The lawyers that used to call did not do so anymore. They did not have any choice, being so dependent on my husband. They were all scared of him.

Soon enough, I received a letter from my husband, forbidding me to come to his office or to call him there. If ever I needed anything, I had to call his secretary; I was even given her private number. It was obvious that he wanted to humiliate me openly. I did not intend to call this fat Bavarian woman asking her for money! Karl was the one who had lost his mind. But maybe he was scared that I would go into his office and take revenge on that promiscuous woman with whom he was now having fun. She was still working as a secretary.

I told Karl one day that his mistress was surely thinking she was in paradise. She should wait and see. A woman that destroys another woman's marriage should know that it brings only bad luck. Karl came towards me, threatening to call the police if ever I tried to hurt the love of his life, his soul mate. He said to me: "You don't want to go to prison, do you?"

I did not intend to have anything to do with that cheap bitch. Why should I bother? She was nothing but a new toy for this disgusting old man. But it amused me that they were scared of me, and were probably looking behind their backs whenever they were in town. This woman thought she had won the game, but she did not know what she had won. My arrogant husband thought he had got rid of me, but he made the mistake of underestimating me; I strongly intended to be a silent fighter, and nibble his brain for at least the next ten years of his life!

To avoid being humiliated by him with those little comments that he loved to make about me, I put an end to those extraordinarily devilish Friday dinners. Paul would have to meet his dad on Saturday mornings instead. Karl could come and fetch him, then he would do his weekly shopping with him, and afterwards they could go to lunch at the Italian restaurant. This was an opportunity for Paul to learn a lot more about his father's new life. His mistress would always call him in the car. Often they argued because apparently she disapproved of Karl taking care of his small son, and was constantly asking whether he had any contact with me. But when Karl would bring his son back, I could see how much he hated me, insulting me for no reason. He wanted me to answer back, provoking me every time he saw me. After that, back in his car, it took him a while before he drove off. Paul, my little guardian angel, soon found out that he was writing down all I had been saying to him. He said to me: "Mum, be careful. Dad called Fabian and told him that soon he will gather enough proof to show that you are insane. He is planning to incarcerate you in a psychiatric hospital for the rest of your life."

I realised that this was my husband's plan; to put me into a mental home in order to have sole custody of Paul and forget me forever. I went to see a solicitor, then another one and another one! I never would have thought how difficult it would be for me to find one; nobody wanted to help me as soon as I said my husband's name. They just said they did not have the time to take my case and that the contract of marriage I had signed held me tight, fists and feet. Finally someone sent me to a lawyer who was approaching retirement and did not seem impressed by my husband's name. He immediately reassured me: "Madam, I can certify at any time that you are in perfect mental health".

Slowly, I made a plan of what to do to get out of this dangerous situation. The first thing was to avoid any contact with him on a day-to-day basis. He still came to have breakfast at our place, whenever he wanted to, because he could not get out of his habits. Like a horse to its shed, he was attached to the house. He wanted to keep control of me. So every morning, he brought his brown bread and his newspaper, and took his seat at the table as if he had the right to do so. But now that I knew about his plan to put me in an asylum, I did not say a word to him. Whenever he came, I shut myself in the bathroom, which was luckily large and comfortable, and I stayed there listening to my French radio until he left the house. I never answered back when I heard him provoke me. I absolutely did not say a word to him. Paul was our mediator; the poor little boy learned very quickly how careful he had to be with what he said to his dad. He was so brave, and did not show him how scared he was of him, always being polite, too polite.

Then I received a letter from Karl on my thirty-fifth birthday. In his letter he told me that he had no obligation to give me any money because of the marriage contract I had signed fourteen years ago. I had renounced of all my rights. But because he was generous, he offered me a monthly alimony. He was not willing to give me any health insurance; he refused to pay for Paul's school lunch, and his bus transport to and from school. I was shocked that Karl refused to pay for his bus, because I did not have a car and his school was thirty kilometres from home. I suppose he wanted me to have no other choice than to send Paul to the public school in our village. In that way he could stop paying the fees for the international school. This would mean that instead of learning in English, Paul would have to do it in German; this sudden change of language would automatically lower his grades. He would lose his friends and the teachers who he loved. Paul was being penalised for being my son, my little boy. Why was this man doing this to his child? Did he really love his son, or did he hold grudges against him because he was not his biological son?

When I read the letter I realised that I would be living on the border of survival from now on. I nearly fainted. But this made me even more determined to fight back!

Really shocking was the fact that Karl was endorsing Paul's monthly child's allocation from the state, but did not give it to me. I never knew that I could have asked for it. He never gave anything for Paul's clothes or food. Keep in mind that I am talking of a multimillionaire solicitor who had twenty-five solicitors working for him. Thinking it was important for Paul to continue having the same life style as before, I accepted being with the tyrant during the school holidays, always skiing in the same shit-hole in Switzerland, or going to those windy north German beaches where everybody would stare at you all the time. During these holidays I endured the humiliations and the insults, depending on his mood. I just shut my mouth. Paul and I had to follow him during his mountain walks and do what he wanted for years and years, even though we were bored to death in his presence. Year after year I tolerated the presence of the devil in my house, and I spent holidays with him, enduring his cruelty because I did not want him to reject his son, Paul. After all, he paid when Paul and I travelled to various cities in Europe, or to the island to visit my parents. At least this was a privilege of which my child would not be deprived. These travels were better than just some more money for our every-day lives. Once again, I was wrong to think that Karl was good to grant us these holidays overseas. Twelve years later, my husband showed me a list of all the debts that I had towards him; every trip had been kept on record, Paul's and mine. So I owed him. The multimil-lionaire had given us nothing at all. But he had imposed his presence in my life for twelve long years after the separation, until God called him to Him.

Chapter 3

Telling about this phase of my life is so hard. All those years I had to fight. I felt exhausted and tremendously sad. But I always perked up, because I had to fight for my son but also because I was proud and was not willing to let him destroy me. The little island girl, the creole, would show him.

So step-by-step, I fought for what was necessary for my son and me. After having succeeded in getting the house in my name, my next project was to ask for my own car. I told the bully that it was essential that I take my son to his same old school. Sending him to another one in the village was not on the agenda. Any refusal and I would go back to the island with my son. With Paul being only nine years old, any judge would give me permission to do so. After weeks of strenuous discussion, the man finally agreed to give me a car.

The third step was to find a job. I went straight to Paul's school director, who knew me personally because I had been working as a volunteer in the library for some years. I asked him if he might have any job for me, and told him about my new situation. Surprisingly, he said he was looking for an assistant in the sports department of the school. In three days, I had a job. The salary was satisfying, and I had solved the issue of Paul's transport to his school. First of all, my solicitor had to ask my husband if he would continue to give me any sustenance at all should I start working. He answered in a signed letter that he would continue to pay me, because he did not believe that I would ever find a job, my German being so poor. He nearly choked when he heard from Paul that I was now working full time at school.

I was replacing a secretary who was retiring, and I had only three weeks to get to learn everything about the job. That's what I did; it was hard work struggling with the computer but I succeeded. The job consisted of multiple tasks and was stressful, but I liked it because it enabled me to meet so many people. I made new friends. I laughed much more than I had before my husband left me. I was going out, even to nightclubs. I started to live as a woman of my age again. This had stopped as soon as I came to live in Germany with a twenty-five years older man and his two volatile and difficult children.

The school required every child to have health insurance before allowing them to travel abroad for various international competitions. I asked Karl to pay for the insurance, but he categorically refused. I knew how much my son was looking forward to the imminent trip to Paris, and started to be very angry with the old man. My voice must have been a little bit louder when I spoke to him; he looked at me with a piercing glaze, as if to hypnotise me, and he said: "Do not talk to me this way. I am God."

I answered back: "You are God's creature, just like everybody else in this world, and I am also a creature of God."

This did not please him at all. This was the rebellious side of me that he disliked so much. In fact he left me because I was no longer submissive. He never paid Paul's health insurance. I paid for it myself, for all the following years until he went to university.

Another time that he was in my kitchen, I told him how I could no longer buy organic fruits because they were too expensive. He answered that for us, Paul and me, the time of fat cows had come to an end. He went on telling me that I should at last try to develop myself spiritually and become a new Theresa Newman, the nun who lived only on water and her everyday Holy Host. I said to him that I was in no way a heretic, and if he thought he was so superior spiritually, why was he not the one living from water and light. I never heard of a saint who needed to accumulate millions like he did. He never gave us money for extra food, but did not hesitate to eat the last piece of cheese or any other food he found in my house without any sense of guilt.

Karl tried over and over again to destroy me. But I had faith in God and I felt protected. One day he came upstairs and knocked at the bathroom, where I was keeping away from him. I did not answer. I heard him breathe heavily like a bull. I had been avoiding the devil for weeks now, but he wanted to see me. I kept silent until eventually the man screamed at me: "Why? Why don't you just disappear from this planet? Why don't you kill yourself and let me live my life in peace?"

But I, proud and stubborn, just kept silent, smiling at myself in the mirror. The man had started to weaken!

Getting a job was winning the first battle in the long war that would continue until my husband's death. He could not bear to know that I had found a job so quickly. He even came to see me at my work place, pretending he wanted to pick up Paul from school. He told Paul that he was surprised; his mum was working in a very beautiful location. My office had windows facing huge chestnut trees on the school grounds. He was even envious of the view!

Owning a car meant freedom and lots of fun for Paul and me. We never stopped going to new places on the weekends, discovering nice little villages. Our friends, mostly Britons and Americans, would tell us about places they had visited and we would go there as well. Sometimes we would join them, forming a group of noisy foreigners, having fun in this cold and deceptively perfect world that was Germany. I was surprised that these foreigners knew a lot more than me, even though I had been living in the country for years. But Karl always went to the same places, never wanting to try something new. I thought how boring my life had been while living with this man for so many years. How I wasted my youth with him!

Chapter 4

After two years, a friend presented me to a man who was a bachelor and rather good-looking. He had a very German name, Boris, and he was more than a decade younger than my husband. Very sociable and agreeable, I noticed immediately that Boris was probably not the most intelligent person. This was very relaxing for me because he had the gift of being humble, and did not try to attract attention constantly. He was the owner of a toyshop that he had inherited from his parents. For some strange reason, the gods were good to Boris. His wishes were granted fairly easily, and he never had to work hard for that. With his good manners and his charisma, he had the affection of the rich and important personalities living near him, and he was regularly invited to all their receptions. Boris was a talented sailor and a member of the nearby yacht club. Soon I was accompanying him there, and found out by the older women's reactions belief that I had stolen their little puppy. They felt animosity towards me; certainly the ugliest women were the worst! Even with their husbands beside them, many of them seemed to think that Boris belonged to them, consciously or unconsciously, secretly wishing to have a love affair with him.

Every weekend we would be at the club sitting at a table, eating the same meals with the same group of people. Their gossip was horrendous; as soon as any of them left the table, there would be someone to talk obnoxiously about him or his wife or children. They would talk about other people's private matters without shame; how this one had lost all his money or how this other man's wife was having an affair with the golf teacher. I would have thought that these people who soi-disant belonged to the high society would have more class. But they had no class at all. Soon, Paul and I got bored and missed our weekends and drove around the country by ourselves.

But going out with Boris was positive for me; I felt reassured in my femininity again. I had someone who liked me and admired me. Boris knew how to make compliments to a woman, and he was always happy to have me by his side. But Boris was also the one who caused the break up of my relationship with my brother.

Leaving me, my husband caused a real emotional avalanche in my life; I lost my biological family at the same time, and it was the worst thing that could happen to me. I found myself brought back to my childhood, when I was holding my arms towards my parents, looking for comfort, but they were not reacting at all. After all these years I finally saw clearly that my family did not feel any love or respect for me. They were too selfish, thinking about themselves and what they had lost materially now that Karl would not offer them any financial backup. In fact, I received more compassion and support from people that I did not really know.

When I called my family to tell them that Karl had left me, my brother reacted as if he had lost his own husband. I had to hear his complaints about how Karl had promised to pay for my niece's studies. He did not stop saying: "He promised, he promised".

That was his only worry. I thought that his daughter was still quite young and she was not that keen on studying anyway. I had to face much more urgent problems: I had my son to feed. Then he told me something which sounded very strange to me; he said: "But how could you, you were a model for me".

I answered back that I never thought I could be a model to him. Was it just because I had married a rich man? That was the silliest thing I had ever heard. Now that I lost a wealthy husband, I was not his model anymore and did not deserve any respect. I was given the bad role again, just like before my marriage! On this island, I was, from now on, considered worthless. I had lost my qualities, my brain and my soul. I was nothing at all because this mad husband of mine had rejected me.

My mother told everybody that my husband had left me because I was so nasty. My father was no support at all; when I talked to him on the phone he stopped me in a cold way: "Ah, you know, I am too old to listen to your problems."

After the separation, I clung to them eight years long, even though they humiliated me and rejected me. The whole family was a group of vultures, and they were attacking me. No one cared about my little boy; they were all so cruel to us. It was as if they could, at last, express openly their real feelings for me. They had no reason to hide their true feelings anymore and they could finally show me that they did not give a damn about me. The other aunts rejoiced openly that I would not be playing the lady anymore. I never thought I was playing anything at all.

I was not surprised to hear that my parents kept in contact with Karl. They never took my side and never reproached him for leaving Paul and me. They were still as friendly as before to him, acting as if nothing happened. But of course, he was the one with the full wallet.

My father never accepted the situation because this was against his principles. Until his death he sent Christmas cards addressed to Mr. Karl S. and family, even if Mr. Karl S. had not been living at this address for years. My father thought that I was the one who did not want to have Karl back because he had an affair. He told me again and again: "You have to forgive".

He refused to hear about the psychological violence that this husband of mine was inflicting on me, that I was constantly being watched and controlled. Karl knew that the only way to keep me under control was financially. My father did not believe me when I told him that Karl was playing a game with me, letting me wait till the last minute before sending me the money for the trip to the island that I had planned with my son. This long wait kept me sleepless and worried. I felt a constant knot in my stomach that largely spoiled the excitement and joy for the anticipated trip with my son. Of course we quickly learned how to trick the man back, hiding the real date of our departure, asking for more money than necessary in case he decided to give us less than what we had asked for. The man blocked me whenever and wherever he could, but I still managed to do everything I wanted. But nobody was interested to hear about our fight against Karl's mad behaviour. This whole misery was just ignored by my parents and relatives. My brother, who I loved, even though he was selfish and despotic, became one of my adversaries. My sister-in-law's reaction did not bother me at all. She never liked me and considered me her milk cow, just good enough to pay for her holidays in Europe and shower her and her daughter with presents.

The loss of my husband was not the end of the world, after all. I had no regrets; he had been such a difficult man to live with, and I did not have the huge burden of taking care of his children anymore. If only Karl had been fair to Paul and me, I would have accepted a divorce, and the whole matter would have been a blessing. Sadly for us, my husband was too nasty to let us live a comfortable life without him. He could not let go; he had to win entirely, just as he had to win all his processes at the tribunal. He had to see my defeat, make me become a wreck; just a diminished, depressed woman like his first wife. But I stayed tough.

Then came the day when I thought it was time for me to present Boris to my parents. Surely they would be relieved to see me no longer alone in a foreign country. Happily, Boris, Paul and I took a flight to the island. I must admit that Boris had been complaining so much about the expensive flight ticket that I paid for it for him, stupid as I was!

Boris and my brother disliked each other the minute they met because they recognised each other; they both liked to live at other people's cost, and they both wanted to take advantage of me as much as possible!

My brother refused to face my new situation; he did not want to change his habits and acted as if I could pay for him and his family as I had always done before. He decided that we absolutely had to go and have dinner in this very expensive restaurant in the south of the island. Before that, we had to go to his place for a drink, causing us to make a long and unnecessary detour. We had taken a taxi. After a drink or two, my brother decided, finally, that it was time to drive to the restaurant. We arrived far too late; there were no tables left. They took us to an artificially made beach, facing the sea. The wind was blowing the guts out of us, and it was really cold. The tropical sun had gone a long time ago. We were given blankets so that we could eat outside, there were some petrol lamps lighting the place but the restaurant itself had no light on anymore. I did no think that the place was as extraordinary as my brother had told us. But I was still curious about the food, because the chef had supposedly been awarded with two Michelin stars. My worries about the bill started as my brother, with a large gesture, asked for one of the most expensive bottles of wine. Boris, not stupid at all, said that he would prefer a bottle of the local beer. I did not drink alcohol, neither did my sister-in-law, so the order for the expensive wine was aborted rather quickly. My brother pulled a face. The whole scene was surreal. We were eating in the strongest wind ever, in the dark, and the sea was black and unfriendly. This evening everything was as dull as my spirit! Later we had to go into the nightclub at the hotel. All the guests had already retired to their rooms. All of a sudden I realized how superficial this all was. We were in a miserable straw hut, with a vulgar disco ball glittering from the ceiling. We had travelled for hours, from the north of the island to the south, to come to such a place, spending all the money I had saved with so much pain. At the hotel in which we were staying, Boris, Paul and I we would have had the nicest of seafood buffets, at a reasonable price. We had missed the music, the friendly guests and staff, just to be dragged to this posh and boring place by my brother. It was my entire fault not being able to say no to him once again!

We had to dance and act as if we were having a lot of fun. While my sister-in-law and my niece were in relatively good moods, I noticed that my brother was getting more and more furious. He seemed to be very angry because he realized that my new boyfriend was not going to be as generous as Karl. Boris wanted to go outside to smoke a cigarette and I went with him, holding hands. We were peacefully admiring the starry sky when my brother came out of the nightclub. He was in one of his fits of rage, his wife and daughter following him anxiously. "Let's get out of here", he shouted at me. "Once more, I was the one who had to pay everything!"

He walked to his car hurriedly, grumbling about us. I told him that Boris and I were only having some fresh air outside. But my brother could not hide his real feelings towards Boris and me anymore. He seemed to be suddenly aware of his financial loss, now that Karl was gone.

After these two years of separation from Karl and all the problems and worries I had faced, I think that I really deserved some nice warm holidays in my country. Paul really deserved it too. I wanted to relax, forget the bad days and be filled with a new energy. I did not intend to play the game of my birth family. Neither did I want to spend all my money in going out to crazy, expensive places just to dote on my brother and his family. It was important for them to show off and lead a life of the vulgar nouveaux riche. It was a tragedy for them that I had lost my husband and with him all the privileges were gone. My brother paid the bill at the restaurant because he wanted to leave in a rush, like a mad man. Of course he gave a very generous tip to the waiters so that they would think that he was a very rich man. But later in the car, he told me that I had to pay him back. I told him immediately that I was willing to pay part of the bill; he had to pay from himself and his family. The answer was: "Well, I have organised this bloody evening for you and now as a thank you, I will have to take a loan at the bank to pay for it."

I answered back : "Do what you have to do. I cannot afford to pay one thousand Deutsch Marks just for one bloody dinner. This is beyond my financial capacities. You should be aware of that."

The same evening he refused to give me my savings book, telling me that if I needed money I only had to ask him as he was in charge of my account. Then he refused to bring me any money at all, telling me that I had hardly any money left. The savings book was my capital, all I had in the island, the money sent for the house expenditures. I felt like I was the hostage of my brother. It was time to put that insupportable situation to an end.

While all this was happening I had to face the fact that my new friend, Boris, was of no help at all; egocentric, only interested in his own well being, I could see that he was not a man on whom I could rely.

Before going back to Germany, I invited all my family to my hotel for coffee. My parents met Boris for the first time. My father did not say a word to him, but at least he stayed polite. My mother, very sociable, as usual, spoke quite well with Boris. When they left, my brother told me that it was his daughter who convinced my father to accept the invitation to meet Boris. My brother could not prevent himself from saying that without his intervention or that of his wife and daughter, my father would never have agreed to meet my new friend. My brother was going on and on with the words; "owing to me, owing to us." Paul told me how the clique was constantly asking him questions about Boris. They wanted to know if he was rich, if he paid for us, if he had a house and which car he was driving. In one word, it was only the financial situation of my new friend that was of importance for them. They forgot to ask whether he was kind and loving to us both, Paul and me.

But then again Paul, at his young age, warned me about Boris; he thought he was no better than the islanders.

Boris had been, indeed, very keen to make me pay everything during our stay on the island. This man was taking advantage of my generosity. Paul was right indeed. I had paid for Boris' flight ticket and hotel accommodation. When we returned back to Germany and we went out for dinner, Boris would always flee to the loo just as the waiter would bring the bill. Even at the cinemas he sent us to queue while he parked the car, and funnily joined us only after I had already paid the cashier. He was so tight that he insisted on using my car all the time, so I had to pay for the fuel. Boris never offered to pay for anything, but he had his high-hatted ways, criticising my food, telling me that what I bought at the supermarket was not of good quality. Well, it was good enough for my son and me. Soon his behaviour eroded my love for him. I was a generous person but not a fool, and I could not accept that a man could think he was so valuable that a woman should pay for his company. Neither did I have motherly inclinations towards him.

Chapter 5

I asked my brother to rent out the house on the island. This was a good way to bring me some extra money for my living; maintaining the house in Germany cost a lot. But month after month my brother told me that no one wanted to rent the house. It was as if no tourists came to the island anymore. Then came the time when my brother refused to answer my phone calls. Talking to his wife was like hitting a wall; she never knew anything; she thought the house was empty for two months or three months, or was that for six months, she did not know exactly. My niece was well trained too; she never knew anything at all. I started to wonder and finally phoned the house at the beach itself. To my surprise, somebody with a foreign accent answered. He told me he had lived in the house for six months already!

I made the mistake of confiding in my mother, telling her how my brother had been lying to me. She must have repeated everything to my brother who insulted me on the phone: "Do you tell people that I am a liar? How dare you? It is not my fault if you are now in the shit!"

I told him that shouting at me did not prevent me thinking, and I asked him to send me the money he had been receiving as a rent for my house. He became aggressive and told me that he had decided to separate my property into two parts. He would go to an attorney and officially become the owner of the house that he had built in front of mine. He was going to do it so that I could sell my house immediately if I wanted. I told him that the share of the land should been done only in my presence and no one else and I sent him a letter ending his power of attorney at once. I flew back there with Paul during the school holidays. Boris wanted to come as well, but this time I refused to pay for him.

As soon as I arrived I went to see my brother to urge him to give me my savings book. Horrified, I saw that he had taken nearly all my money. The transaction had actually been done only three days after I informed him that my husband had left me. I asked for explanations; he told me that I asked him to give all the money to the church! How would have I told him to give money to the church when I was terrified of not having enough for my son and myself? My brother started shouting at me again, called me humiliating names, threatening to slap me in the face. He never gave me my money back.

An ex-colleague of mine advised me to go to an attorney. I arranged for an appointment to see the man without delay, asking my brother to join me. After all, he was the one asking for his part of the plot of land at the beach. This attorney was a creole like me. Tanned but really dark, small and thin, I thought he looked mediocre in his small dusty office. On the wall, in full view, was hung a picture of a little boy with round cheeks and big green eyes. "Oh, yes", I said to myself, "the European genes had come out of the grandson. Congratulations. If the child had turned out dark, he surely would not have had a picture of himself exhibited right in the middle of his grandpa's office."

The conman, the attorney, did not seem delighted to see me. Louis came to join us immediately after I entered the office; he must have been waiting for me, watching from a car. I soon stumbled on what has been going on behind my back. Unluckily for me, the two men knew each other quite well. Hands were shaken; there were claps of the shoulders. I heard one saying to the other; "Hello, old devil, how's life? How are the kids doing? And the wife?"

This was inevitable. Both the attorney and my brother belonged to that clique of creoles who clung to their European origins and presented them on a golden tray. They deeply regretted their mixed blood, looking at the white people with envy. They spoke constantly of their European ancestors, ignoring the African or Indian, Arabian or Madagascan part of them, regretting to have the genes that gave them their tanned skin or their too flat nose or their frizzy hair.

I had given the name and address of the attorney to my brother the day before. It was clear that they had already spoken to each other. God knows what my brother must have told the man in order to manipulate him against me. My brother was a true genius of manipulation. Everybody liked him and believed him. My questions seemed to annoy both of them. It was my brother who was replying to me, cutting short any of the attorney's explanations. My brother was breathing loudly, angry with me. Then he started to shout at me again, treating me as 'mad' because I was asking again and again to have the money back that he had stolen from my account. He told the attorney to call an ambulance to take me to the psychiatric hospital. The attorney stayed put, at least acting professionally. I stayed calm myself, and stayed focused on the share of the plot of land. I wanted to keep as much land for me as possible. I was trying to think rationally even if my brother was screaming at me. He said in front of this stranger: "Karl has all my compassion. I understand now why he had to kick you in the ass and throw you on the street, out of his life".

Not a word from the attorney, the man was dumb; then he explained to me that the property was originally owned by a society, and all of the shares except for one belonged to me. It would be better to sell the society as it was, because it was too complicated to divide it into parts. It meant that everything had to be sold, including my brother's house. I sensed that my brother was no longer interested in dividing the plot of land. He wanted everything to stay as it was before, enabling him to rent his house, still having access to all the grounds and to my house. I had to think clearly and very quickly. I thought that if everything stayed as before, my brother would continue to rent my house without giving me any money. I thought that selling the house would not be disadvantageous to me after all. I also wanted to put an end to any dependence on my brother. I took a deep breath and said to the attorney: "Well, I shall sell everything."

I left the office. Everything looked so unreal, as if I was on stage with a role in a drama. But seeing that my brother's anger was getting out of bounds, I realised that no, this was all real. Even my life might be in danger. I went down the narrow stairs, walking slowly, followed by my brother. I knew he could do anything to me. His footsteps were loud, he kept screaming at me. I could only hear the words: whore, slut. He threw something at me but I rushed outside in the bright sunny light and saw my taxi waiting for me at the gate. As if the driver knew that I was in trouble, he drove off in a hurry. On my way back to the hotel, surrounded by the most colourful and luxurious vegetation, I thought that my brother had taken the mask off his face, disclosing nothing but his hate and greed. I would have to fight for my rights now.

The next day, Paul and I left Boris at the hotel and paid a visit to my parents. I thought I could complain about my brother, but neither my father nor my mother showed any interest in listening to me. They kept stubbornly silent. Paul did not receive an affectionate hug or a comforting word from his grandparents, even though they knew that the child was going through a hard time. I realised later why they were behaving so strangely. My brother had already talked to them, telling them that I had gone completely mad, asking for money that I never had. It was all in my head. I was totally paranoid to think that he would have stolen my money. In fact, Karl was the one who engendered this fantastic rumor about my madness. He told my brother that he had to leave me because I was so aggressive and jealous; living with me had become impossible. My brother took the chance and used the same argument against me. I am sure that if I had gone to the island without Boris, my brother would have succeeded in having me incarcerated in a psychiatric hospital. He would not have hesitated to, with Karl's blessing of course. These two liars had destroyed my reputation on the island. This 'madness' of mine stuck to me as a stigma for all those years. My mother was the only one who knew that my brother was a liar; she also knew that I was not mad. But she never came to my rescue; she could not contradict my brother. She loved him too much.

My father was desperate, because he had doubts about my sanity. My mother was mentally ill, so he thought I was following in her line. This made him very sad for years, and I will never forgive Karl or my brother for what they did to the old man. He had suffered enough with my mother. It was only seven years later, a few weeks before he passed away, that I managed to have a convincing and sincere talk with him. I told him what really had happened between my brother and me. But it was too late; evil had won for years on the island.

Before I returned to Germany I called a surveyor, who valued the two houses at the beach. I was determined to play fair with my brother and pay him the exact value of his house, as soon as the property was sold. I wanted to put an end to my relationship with my brother, but I did not want to take revenge for what he did to me. I could feel his fear of losing everything, and I felt sorry for him.

Shortly after the entire dramatic situation at the attorney's office, I received a phone call from a woman whom I vaguely knew, but who was a very good friend of my brother's. She was an estate agent, a vulture, determined to force me to sign a contract with her. She harassed me on the phone, exaggerating the price she could get for the property. I stayed polite but was very distant, because I knew that she must have made a deal with my brother. She could take years to sell the houses, allowing my brother to rent both of them in the meantime. I told her I had to think about her proposition, and returned to Germany without contacting her. But as soon as I got home I received a facsimile from her wanting me to sign a document. I answered back that I did not intend to do so because she was my brother's friend. She insisted that there had been a gentleman's agreement between us. I told her to go to hell.

I managed to find a tenant for my house until it was sold. I knew it would take a long time before I found someone willing to buy two houses at once. I asked a friend and ex-colleague of mine, Madeline, to help me as a representative. I needed somebody to do the bank transactions, sending the rent to Germany. I thought that the woman would be happy to help me because she would receive a bonus from the rent. I had given a lot of presents to this woman and her son, even paying all the costs of her divorce some years ago. Everything went well for the first few months. I received the rent every month, which allowed me to pay all my bills and live a decent life with my son. I could even replace the old boiler in the house. But then the woman started to take her time before sending me any payments.

Sometimes I had to wait for eight weeks or more. I had to call her constantly to ask what was happening. She said that she did not have time to do it because she was too busy. The bank was just beside her office, a few steps away! I felt that there was something wrong with the woman. She started to quote the Bible endlessly. She advised me to turn the right cheek to my brother and make peace with him. Apparently he had started to telephone her, and since then she prayed for him. Madeline had recently left the Catholic Church to join a sort of sect, which caused a complete transformation in her personality. I told her that to turn my cheek would make me my brother's victim. I was not born to be a victim.

One day she told me that my tenant had to be thrown out of my house. She could ask my brother to help her and they both would do it, if I gave them permission. She said that my brother had found out that the tenant was constantly having prostitutes in my house. I answered that the man was free to do as he wanted, and a diplomat from the French embassy would never want to attract his neighbour's attention with such dubious behaviour. I told her that my brother was the instigator of the story, trying to take over my house again for the rent.

Madeline contacted several estate agents for me, but she felt she had the right to divulge my private life to these strangers. I was extremely upset when one of the agents called me and told me how much he pitied me for all my problems; it seemed that I had no luck in my life. I assured him that he was wrong; I would never swap my life with his, or that of my friend. I did not think that my life was mediocre at all, compared to that of most of the islanders I knew, imprisoned in their little ghetto, clutching each other in their families even if they were absolutely unhappy. They had to have the safety of not being alone.

I finally found an agent myself, contacting the agent who sold us this same property ten years before. He was an experienced man, more interested in his fees than in listening to my brother's lies about me.

Chapter 6

Not only did I have to solve the problems with my brother and my house, I also had to face those with Karl, who had become my worst enemy. He had stopped his provocations because I refused to play his game, hiding when he came home. He was still watching me very carefully, waiting for me to show any sign of weakness, ready to take my son away and stop paying me any alimony. He must have heard that there was a man in my life, because for some time he had started paying us visits at the most incongruous hours and days. One Sunday morning he nearly came face to face with Boris at my house. Boris was in the kitchen, preparing coffee. Paul and I were getting ready to go out for brunch with friends in a restaurant at a lake. Karl still had the house key, and I heard him open the door and call Paul by his name. Karl lived in a nearby village and could easily come to our place. Paul reacted very quickly; he ran downstairs and rushed to the door. Without giving his father any chance to come in, he said we were going out and kissed him good-bye. Karl said that he would come back another time and left the house. Paul and I went to see poor Boris in the kitchen. He was still holding a cup of coffee in his hand, hiding behind a cupboard, really scared. We had a good laugh, but I was relieved that Karl had not seen Boris. I was sure he would have punished me for having a friend, and the only way to do so would have been to stop giving me any money at all.

Paul was very good at school, surrounded by very good teachers. The music teacher was the best. She was an adorable woman who just loved her job. The children were fond of her and she dedicated herself entirely to music. Luckily for Paul, in that difficult year for him, he had the chance to take part in various international school concerts. So they travelled from Paris to Zurich and Vienna. They took part in a television show, and sang with a very famous singer at the Olympic station in Munich, in front of ten thousand spectators. The children had a wonderful time, and this helped Paul to overcome his feelings of sadness and fear.

But then Karl left an envelope on the breakfast table at our house 'by accident'. It was open, and Paul had a look inside. He showed me the medical report about Karl. The urologist confirmed Karl's inability to have children. There was a list of sperm banks in foreign countries and other donors if he wished to have a child with his partner. Paul looked at me and said: 'That's it, Mum. Dad wants to replace me.'

My heart broke to see my little boy crying. He was horrified by what his father was doing. I had to stay strong, but deep inside I felt as if my heart was shrinking, it hurt. The pain continued for months; sometimes I had to keep my breath shallow. I was a boxer in the ring, avoiding the punches of my adversary. But I did not stop; I could not because of my little boy.

Karl never had a child with that woman. One day out of the blue he told me how I refused to have a child from him. I told him that he was mistaken; I had given him the most beautiful child ever. He jumped backwards, taken aback to have revealed one of his many secrets; he had got confused with the many women in his life. I looked at him with disdain.

Chapter 7

Boris was getting on my nerves. A real hypochondriac, he spent hours going from doctor to doctor. Because he had seen a tiny spot on his left cheek he hurriedly went to consult his dermatologist. He was so excited to have found something unusual on his skin. One of Boris's best friends was a general practitioner; after a talk with him, he assumed that his friend's advice to go to a cardiologist was a sign that the man had seen something wrong with him; maybe because he was out of breath while they were out walking together. So Boris went to see a cardiologist and underwent all the tests with enthusiasm. Boris kept on finding problems in his body. Following his obsessive attitude towards health, he persuaded his mother to have a colonoscopy. I thought that such a procedure was unnecessary; for a woman of her age, she was very healthy. The probability of finding something unusual in her intestines was very high. I was right. The doctors found a little cyst and decided to operate on her quickly, God knows why. Before the surgery, this eighty-eight year old woman could drive her own car to go shopping and meet her friends in a cafe, cook and do her housework all by herself. But as she regained consciousness after the operation, she was unrecognisable; she had lost her mind, and was completely confused and aggressive towards the nurses. She caught an infection at the hospital, and her condition went from bad to worse. I went to see her every day because Boris could not visit a hospital by himself. I accompanied Boris's mother in her agony, until her death. She did not really know what was happening to her. She kept telling me that she had seen Boris's father, her husband, wearing a beautiful while pullover. He was even there beside her while we were standing at her bed. The man had died a decade ago. I felt how life was playing strange tricks on me. Every day I was at the bedside of this woman who was a stranger, caring for her. I was very aware that I would never be able to do the same for my own mother and father. They would die without me at their side. But maybe they did not need me; my brother would have the privilege of being there for them. Boris's mum died after six weeks. I was grateful to her for her warmth and friendliness towards Paul and me.

Shortly after his mother's death, Boris went through a complete metamorphosis. In a way, I think it liberated him to lose his mother, the closest person to him. He had kept a secret from her and now that she was no more, he could reveal it without the fear of hurting her. Boris was very touchy, moody; there was something very feminine about him. He became very jealous of Paul, criticising the child for everything he did. Paul was very good with the computer, and Boris began asking him for help, but then he would shout at the child, saying he was too fast. If anything went wrong with the computer, it would always be Paul's fault. The worst was when Boris tried to educate the child. He thought he had great ideas and wanted to change things. I tried to explain to him that Paul had his own father, I did not need anyone to interfere in his education. Boris told all his friends about everything the child was doing. He thought Paul was too fat; the child had put on some weight after Karl had left us. This was a normal reaction; Paul was still very good at school but expressed his frustration and fear by eating more than usual. I was aware of that but left the child in peace, knowing he needed time to get resettled. But Boris did not agree with me; he kept talking about it with his clique at the yacht club. He said that Paul was fat and greedy. At the club there was always an idiot who would tell Paul to stop eating. Then a woman came to see me; she was one of the witches who did not want me to be at Boris's side. She told me how she heard about my problem.

"What problem?" I asked, surprised.

"Boris has told me Paul has put on weight. I have a friend who is a nutritionist. She could help him to lose weight. I could call her right now, there is no time to lose."

I thought I was wasting my time with this stupid woman in front of me. Who did she think she was, interfering in my life like that? I asked her if she really thought that Paul was fat. She said not really, but he was so skinny before, one could see the difference. I then asked her if she also had a friend who was a psychologist, because I could send Boris to him. The problem was not Paul, but Boris, who was acting like a silly cow; he could not stop gossiping. The woman sensed danger, and turned tail without asking for more. After that I felt that the clique did not want me at the yacht club anymore, except for a few who knew me from the school. But nobody dared to say anything about Paul again. As I said before, my little boy lost his kilos gradually, as soon as he felt that I was getting on better and that our life without his dad was harmonious and easy-going.

But Boris did not stop trying to be the man of the house. Paul liked to do his homework lying flat on the rug in front of the fireplace, with his books spread out in front of him. I would watch television, without disturbing him. His notes were very good indeed. Amour, the dog lay close to him. Paul did his homework and I helped him from time to time. I liked the peaceful atmosphere of those evenings. When Boris started to come regularly, he wanted to change everything. He said that my son should be doing his homework on a writing table in his bedroom. He ordered him to go to his room, but I interfered. Of course Boris discussed it at the club. But this time one of his friends, who was a retired teacher, told him to leave the boy in peace; he should do his homework wherever he wanted. Boris, stupid as usual, could not help repeating his friend's words to me. I told him again to stop discussing my child with the rest of the world. My son had his own father and he did not need another one.

Some weeks later, after dinner, I left Boris and Paul in the living room to clean up the kitchen. I did the cleaning hastily because I did not have a nice feeling about leaving them together. Entering the room I found Boris alone, lying comfortably on the sofa. I asked him where Paul was, thinking that he might have gone to his room to pick up a book. Boris told me, with a victorious smile on his stupid face, that Paul had finally gone to his bedroom, where he should be. I went upstairs and saw my son on his bed, staring at the ceiling, with big tears rolling down his cheeks. My son just said to me:

"Mum, your friend is so stupid."

He said no more. I could not bear to see my child so sad. I had sworn to myself to give him his childhood back. I wanted him to laugh and jump and be happy. Boris was no help at all; on the contrary, he was a tic on my back, a hindrance to my son's happiness. I had to get rid of that man. My child was the most important person in my life. I told Paul not to worry; I was going to solve this small problem immediately. I went down the stairs and talked to Boris. I told him that I was not willing to have a relationship with someone who had a problem with my child. I urged him to leave my house. But Boris would not let me go, and acted as if there was nothing wrong between us. I did not want to share my life with this man anymore. I was determined of getting rid of him, and had to think of a good strategy. It did not take me long to decide what to do. I stopped spoiling him with his everyday treats; I did not shop at the Italian delicatessen anymore, no more expensive wine, no Italian ham and cheese, no more tortellini and fresh pasta. When he asked for his expensive shampoo I acted as if I was deaf, buying only the things that Paul and I needed and liked. Boris complained about the poor quality of my food. I told him to do the shopping himself. He never thanked me, and never thought of paying for the food he was eating at my place. I was feeding him. He was shocked to hear me asking for his contribution to the expenses; he thought that giving me the honour of his presence was more than enough.

After two months, Boris had the splendid idea of renting his mother's flat. He was always trying to make some money. One of his numerous friends had separated from his wife and was looking for a *pied à terre*. So Boris offered him his mum's tiny apartment for rent. It was just part of Boris's house. When I paid a visit to Boris at his place, Mathias, the tenant was always there. The man was a gourmet; he cooked every weekend, apparently the most fabulous and expensive dishes. Boris stopped coming to my place for dinner. He said Mathias had invited him to share his meals. I was very relieved to have my peaceful evenings with my son again. Boris was not there to annoy my son anymore. But when he disappeared for three weeks without saying where he was, I thought there was something weird going on. One Sunday morning I went to see him without warning. I saw the two men in their dressing gowns, standing very close to each other. I felt an intimacy between them. It surprised me. The way they reacted when they saw me made me become even more suspicious. Mathias bent his head and really avoided looking me in the eye, he then stole out of the room like a thief. Boris did not know what to say. All of a sudden everything became clear. The men were lovers.

I returned home, packed Boris's things in a bin bag, took them to his house, and left them at the entrance gate. Later that day Boris called me, asking me why I did this to him, he had done nothing wrong. I told him that I did not want to share my life with a bisexual. I wished him good luck in his new relationship. Thank God I could get rid of him. My life was much better without this moody man. Paul felt free at home again.

Months later Boris told me that his friend Mathias had left him, refusing to pay the rent. I told him that it was fair enough, after all Mathias had fed him for seven months with the most expensive and exquisite food. Why should he pay the rent? Boris was not very happy with my way of seeing things. After that he called me one day and asked me to accompany him to hospital for a checkup. This time I refused categorically, I was not willing to do anything for him anymore.

Boris never forgot me, calling me regularly, curious to know if I was in a relationship or not. Sometime after, he dated an elderly married woman. He was always looking for a woman who had enough money to spoil him. He also had love affairs with younger men, hiding his double life from his friends but keeping up the hope of starting a new relationship with me.

Chapter 8

———◆———

Time was passing by, and I heard nothing about the sale of the property on the island. It seemed that there was nobody willing to buy a plot of land with two houses. The estate agent told me that my brother was putting off all the potential buyers who came to visit the houses. His tenants were helping him. They were afraid to have to leave the house.

After a year and a half, I asked my estranged husband Karl, to accompany me to the island. We had to go there to see what was really going on. This time I felt it would be better if Karl would come with me. Karl agreed to come with us, Paul and me. I think his instinct as a lawyer was stronger that his bad feelings for me. He felt he had to make sure that the money was saved; after all the money was not only mine, it was our son's too.

Once again we stayed in one of these paradisiac resort hotels. Once again, the bright light and the turquoise sea struck me. The vivid coloured flowers and the white, hot sand looked unreal to me, out of place in contrast to my state of mind. I felt so sick to know that this beautiful scenery was just decoration. I did not belong to this environment at all. Everything nice and beautiful had been removed, pulled away from me. There was nothing left but my brother's hatred because he could not use me anymore. I promised myself never to return to this country again. It was better for me to live amongst the Germans; at least they did not hide their feelings behind a mask, and they did not think I was worthless because my husband had left me.

Madeline had spoken negatively of my tenant. I wanted to meet him, to have my own opinion. So one evening I went to see him, and Karl came with me. The French diplomat did not know we were coming. The gentleman let us into the house and presented us to his wife, a beautiful young woman with extremely good manners. She told me that she had been with her husband all the time. It confirmed my feelings that this whole story about the prostitutes had been made up by my brother. The next day I called Madeline and told her about it. But the woman had a fit of rage and shouted at the phone: "Anyway, you will never be able to sell these bloody houses. Put that into your head once and for all."

I was stupefied by the strange reaction of the woman who was supposed to be my friend. She was on my brother's side now, wishing me bad luck for the sale of my property. But all this did not stop me. On the contrary, my determination was strengthened. How she had changed, poor Madeline. She never stopped referring to the bible; ever since she joined the religious sect. I did not trust those who talked about God all day long. Madeline was the only one in her family who lived on the island. All her siblings had immigrated to Australia; even their old parents joined them after some years. Some months before, Madeline told me about her wish to go and visit them; she complained about the expensive flight and other costs for the trip. I offered to pay for half of her flight ticket. She reacted very badly to my offer, disappointed that I was not paying everything for her and for her son. She said how his grandparents were longing to see him. I told her that her siblings could contribute towards his flight ticket. I was determined not to pay for the young man who had been very impolite to me on the phone, sighing loudly when I asked to talk to his mother. Once I heard him say to his mother:

"Your friend from Germany is on the phone. You will have to listen to her rubbish for hours now."

He certainly knew that I could hear him.

Madeline took the money from my bank account, but her thank you did not seem very enthusiastic. After that, she changed towards me. As soon as she returned from her trip, which she undertook without her son, she sent me a letter informing me that she did not want to be my representative anymore. Here I was again, losing a friend because I was not willing to grant her all of her wishes. Like everybody else on this bloody island, she thought I should give away all my money, disregarding my own needs. Reading the bible did not stop her feeling jealous of me. What happened with these people? They were the most materialistic individuals that I had ever met in my life.

After consulting the estate agent, Karl decided to have a serious talk with my brother who agreed to talk to him, but insisted that he should meet him alone. I was determined to see him and talk to him too. After all, he was the one who wanted to divide the plot of land. This not being possible, I had to sell everything. If he had been fair towards me, his only sister, this would never have happened. But my brother met Karl alone. Karl literally ran away from me; my brother must have told him something on the phone to convince him that it was crucial that he came alone. My brother told Karl about Boris, my lover, who came with me twice to the island. He told him that we were living together. Karl denied it because he would have seen him; he came to my house regularly. My brother said this to my husband while knowing perfectly that I had a catastrophic contract of marriage, making me completely dependent on Karl's goodwill. My brother wanted to destroy me, he wanted to see me and my son me thrown on the street, without any financial resources. He did not know that I had a job, and that the house in Germany belonged to me.

My father warned me, he was scared for me. He had heard my brother telling his wife and my mother how he had revealed my hidden life to my husband. He even said:

"Let's wait and see what happens to her, this slut." According to my poor dad, my brother was rubbing his hands with anticipation while speaking to them.

When I heard that, I was really afraid of my husband's reaction. How could my own brother betray me in such a way? He had stolen my money and told everybody that I was mad, but I would never have imagined that he could go that far to crush me down. I saw how evil he was, without scruples or the faintest feeling of guilt. I could not imagine how much my brother must have hated me all those years.

But as always happens in these situations, instead of doing me wrong, my brother changed the whole situation in my favour. He did not take into account that Karl, my husband, could act quite irrationally sometimes. I returned to Germany carrying a new load of fear and worry on my shoulders, anticipating the worst. But actually there was a change in Karl's behaviour and not what I had expected; I noticed that Karl came more often to see us, even on weekdays. Maybe my brother's tales made him think about the eventuality that I was now ready to start a new life with someone else, and that I would get rid of him. One day he came to see me in the kitchen and asked me:

"What would you say if I came back home?"

I was really stupefied, but I thought it was a ruse; I had to be very careful. Maybe he wanted to see my reaction, and eventually force me to tell him about Boris. But Boris was not sharing my life anymore and I was not dating anybody else. So I said to him:

"Only if you promise me not to have any more contact with that woman."

He answered: "I cannot promise you such a thing. Maybe she'll need me one day."

I knew my husband too well; this was his typical answer. He wanted to show me he still had the power to do as he liked.

So as naturally as I could, I said to him: "Well, just stay where you are then and leave me in peace."

I did not intend to live with a man that saw his ex-lover whenever she needed him. What would she need him for? Would it be for physical contact, for financial help, or to heal her soul? How would I react in such a situation? Should I accept that woman in our life and just lower my eyes with submission? It was not in my nature to live that way, and I was determined not to let this ugly old man humiliate me again. Never ever again.

When I told him that he might come back, I was thinking rationally, not out of love. There was absolutely no love left in my heart for that man. I wanted to test him, see what he had to offer me, maybe a fairer contract of marriage. This would have meant the end of my financial worries, a higher standard of living. But God knows whether the old fish would have bitten the bait. Finally, I was happy that he answered me the way he did, telling me clearly that he intended to go on seeing the woman again. I was too proud to accept this sort of concession. If he had at least told me that he still loved me and he was sorry for the harm he had caused us, Paul and me, I would have thought twice before destroying his illusions. But he would never admit that he had been mistaken, nor would he ever apologise for his horrible behaviour. He had said so many hurtful things to me, that it had been ten whole years since he had felt any love for me, that he had at last met his soul mate in that woman and that with me, our relationship was only for the sex. My energy was so negative, he said once, if he had stayed with me, it would have destroyed his health.

This man was nuts. I hardly had any sex with him. He wanted to attain enlightenment by refusing to have any normal sex life with me. I was so young, so beautiful and I was longing for some physical contact, some warmth with a real man. But I stayed loyal to this old demon, even though there had been opportunities to betray him. I felt so stupid. His hurtful words left an indelible stain on my heart; I had given him the most beautiful child, even though he was a weak sterile man. It was an act of love. But this act of love had faded from his mind completely. My loyalty to him and my devotion were worthless, just details.

If I was neither his great love nor his soul mate, he should go and let me live my own life. I knew at that time how strong I was, that I had come a long way without him; I could continue to do so because I was doing fine by myself. After all, I had no intention of going back to the past, living an everyday routine in a house transformed into a sterile monastery. Every day, he ate this horrible macrobiotic food and every morning he rinsed his mouth with sunflower oil. I was not allowed to open my mouth during breakfast, nor listen to the radio. I did not want to have his horrible children on my back again. No, I was wrong to cry that much when he left me; my life was much better without him. Even Paul did not want his father back:

"No, Mum, I love my life now. I do not want him here, he will spoil everything."

Six months after this journey to my country, I succeeded in selling my property. What a relief and what a victory. I would not have to go back there and face those nasty people anymore. Not even a stay in a luxurious hotel attracted me. You could not lie on the beach and relax; hawkers constantly harassed you, trying to sell you towels and other silly things. Their eyes fixed on the breasts of the white women, they would bend their bigs head too close to them; and when they were told to get off, they became insolent and mocking. I asked my husband to help me once more and he agreed to go to the island without me this time, and represent me for the sale of the property. Karl did not engage the attorney, my brother's friend, to do the contract, he asked the buyers to take on their own. Karl gave my brother a fair amount of money, representing the exact value of the house he built on my grounds. Instead of putting an end to the quarrel, my brother spit his poison in Karl's face and said how much he hated me. He asked for more money, but Karl reminded him that he had rented his house for twelve years. He also reminded him that during those twelve years his tenants had prevented us from enjoying our own garden and beach; we had become strangers in our own home.

Chapter 9

———◆———

Shortly after my husband left me, a friend of mine told me to call a psychic for advice. Instead of being depressed and starting taking pills or drinking alcohol, I asked a psychic for help. I was lucky; she was a genuine, reliable woman who, after some years, became a friend. She gave me tremendous support during all that time. It was this woman who opened my eyes and showed me that the members of my family back home, my friends, all of whom I loved sincerely, were in fact, just taking advantage of me.

Mary was in her forties but looked much younger. An elegant, loving wife and mother, she had both feet on the ground and was managing her household with dexterity and diplomacy. But during the evening she would sit in front of her tarot cards and her spirit would travel in a different world. I took years to believe in her, I could not or would not, because she gave me a hideous depiction of the members of my family. This was too upsetting. However, as time passed, my relatives showed me how indifferent they were to the constant struggle of my life. I could see their selfishness and greed for even more money; a real plague, gangrene on their soul.

I was convinced of Mary's psychic gift when, one year after being acquainted with her, I received a letter from the court, informing me of the date of my divorce. Paul and I had spent some days in Italy. I was very thin and still felt quite miserable. This letter brought me to real despair. I called Mary and told her about the letter; the divorce was to be pronounced in some weeks. My heart was thumping, I could barely breathe. Mary answered me, all jovial and with her crystal voice told me:

"But there will never be a divorce."

I insisted: "Mary, it says the 9th of September. It's over. He will divorce me and not give me a penny."

Mary repeated: "I do not see any divorce. Calm down. Speak to your husband and ask him to wait until Paul has reached his majority."

Without real conviction, I spoke to my husband. To my surprise, he agreed. We did not divorce. I thank God for sending me an angel to give me support and advice. Mary told me things that were horrible to hear. She thought my sister-in-law, Shirley, was a demon. She repeated many times: "This woman could not bear to see you happy. The more you covered her with presents, the more she wished you misfortune. She indulges in black magic, just like her grandmother. She has control over your brother, your parents, your friends. She put an end to your marriage. She goes regularly to a witch who tells her about your life. Every time you are getting better, she pays the witch to do you harm. You have to protect yourself."

I lost too much time before protecting myself. I was a devoted Catholic, and I just could not believe that my sister-in-law was such an evil person. But with the obstacles coming again and again in my life, I finally decided to believe in Mary's words. When I was a child my nanny used to tell me stories about African and Indian voodoo. Sometimes at road junctions you could see offers of flowers, coconuts, citrus fruits and other things, put there by a witch as a ritual against or for someone. Black magic still existed in the island even though nobody talked openly about it. During our last holidays at the island, my husband and I saw one of these offerings in our garden, on one of the steps leading to the beach. Karl picked up one of the fruits and a friend of ours told him vigorously not to touch anything. Some months after, my husband left me.

I noticed that a day or two after each telephone call that I made to my parents, something unpleasant happened to me. I knew that my mother gave an account of everything I said to my brother and his wife.

There was also my cousin Josephine, who I loved like a sister. Her children were causing her so much worry, and I used to call her regularly to give her some moral support. She was different from me, giving importance to things that seemed trivial to me. She loved gossiping, and was always eager to hear any exciting story that she could tell her friends and relatives. One day she asked me whether Karl hit me when he heard that I had a lover. I told her that my husband never hit me, and his reaction to my brother's betrayal had turned out very positively for me. I did not know she would tell my brother. I thought she was still on my side, because she did not like my brother's wife. But three days after the telephone call, Karl came to our house. He was acting as if the devil had taken over him; he was very aggressive towards me and provoked me. I was not vigilant enough in the presence of my enemy and answered back just as aggressively. We had a terrible fight; he even tried to slap me. I sensed, at the last moment, that I had to back off. But it was too late, and afterwards I lived in fear for my future, regretting bitterly having let the fight happen. This might have destroyed all the fragile harmony that I had created, with so much pain and patience, between my husband and I. Josephine had two faces; she lied to me, telling me that she did not see my brother at all. But the psychic, Mary, swore that they kept in regular contact. I could not deny any longer that my cousin was a hypocrite. I knew my family had a habit of speaking ill of everybody else, but I never listened to them. I tolerated their little weaknesses because I could not forget how Josephine and Juliet, my aunt, cared for me when I was a little girl rejected by my own mother. These strange happenings confirmed Mary's affirmations but to be aware of Josephine's insincerity towards me was a new source of sadness.

Even though Mary had opened my eyes, it took me years to accept the fact that for me, nothing good was coming from the island. I had to unchain myself, erase any feeling of duty towards my parents and other relatives, because they were taking advantage of this. I decided to act as if they did not exist anymore; this was not easy at all because I still loved them. Like a baby who was learning to walk, I started, little by little, to distance myself from the island and detach myself from my family. I stopped calling them regularly, sometimes waiting for two months. There were many complaints from Josephine, who urged me to call my mother at least once a week. But neither my cousin nor my parents ever thought of calling me or writing to me to ask me how Paul and I were getting on.

All those fourteen years, while I shared my life with this crazy husband of mine, I had thought of nothing but to grant my parents, brother and other relatives all their wishes. It took me so much energy and so much pain to beg for Karl's financial support. When Karl left me, I had nothing, no car, not jewelry, and no money in my bank account in Germany. I had just a white bicycle to enable me to go shopping at the nearby supermarket. Each time I asked my husband for a considerable amount of money, it was for one member of my family who was in absolute need of a new car or for some other luxurious desire. I never asked for anything special for me; I had been giving priority to these monsters, hoping for some love. My husband's money did not turn my head; I did not really have a huge desire for material things, my only luxury had been to travel a lot in Europe and visit museums.

Now it was time to think about my son and myself. I became aware that my generosity was too boundless, in reality; it caused my relatives and friends to become more and more greedy, more and more dissatisfied.

Chapter 10

Paul had reached his fifteenth birthday; he travelled from time to time with his schoolmates to other international schools in Europe to take part in debates and choir competitions. One day, returning from London, he told me with great enthusiasm about the boarding school where he had been staying. He said how nice it had been to live with other students of his age. He contacted a girl friend, Evelyn, who had recently changed schools and was now going to a well-known boarding school near the Lake of Constance. Evelyn invited him to visit her at school. I thought it would be very positive for my son to be among young people and have some distance from his oppressive father and me. I wanted him to enjoy his last years as a teenager, to be able to act foolishly sometimes and have fun with his friends. His father immediately took Paul's idea to heart; he did not mind paying the higher fees. Karl was, in fact, unusually excited about this matter – too excited. I was not a fool; I knew that he secretly wished to hurt me by taking my son away from me. We all went together to visit the school. To my surprise, Karl had already arranged an interview with the school director. Paul was told that his results were so good that he was immediately accepted and could start at his new school in the coming week, if he wanted to. He was given a few days to make his decision. I told Paul that he should not worry about me. He thought about it for two days, and then decided to change schools. Karl was surprised and disappointed by my reaction; he wanted to see me absolutely devastated. He thought he would create conflict between my son and me. But he was wrong, none of this would ever happen.

At first, it was not very easy for me to live in an empty house. But I was sure that I had made the right decision for Paul, and this helped me. Even Paul felt a bit lost at first, but soon he became more independent. I also had to hear some disagreeable comments from some mothers, appalled that I sent my son to a boarding school. But I told them that it was not a punishment; I wanted to prepare my son for adulthood. Want it or not, a child grows up, and like a bird he leaves his nest one day. This separation did not alter our good relationship; on the contrary, it strengthened it. When Paul came home on the weekends, it was bliss. We were happy, having so many things to tell each other. Paul never rebelled against me. Even though we argued sometimes, we made peace very quickly. What pleased me most was that Paul made nice friends in his school, friendships that turned into brotherhood because these boys and girls, who were far away from their families, shared their friends' joys and sadness and could count on each other for support.

I started a new life as a single woman. I had a few brief love affairs, but I found out after some years that I was at my best when I did not have a man in my life. I was too strong, too independent, and no longer willing to be submissive in any way. I was quite unlucky not to have met any good men. The men I met were all selfish, with big egos that had to be flattered and reassured day after day. I did not want to let anybody hurt my son, be jealous of him, and criticise everything he was doing or saying. All of my boyfriends ended up considering him their rival. Without a man, I was free. Life was great without the constant fear of no longer being loved by a man. I was grateful to be leading my life as it was.

Karl had become my personal gardener! He came regularly, spending hours in my garden. Unable to let go, he still considered my house as his. I let him do as he wished; it was all to my advantage. He came during the whole summer, started to work, kneeling down to weed, or cutting the roses, revealing his distorted backbone in the sunshine. I would watch him from my window, but never went outside to talk to him. I put an end to these horrible ski holidays with him. I broke my ankle while cross country-skiing one day; it happened on an easy, flat track, but I had my husband behind me, stealing all my energy like an old vulture. He was getting on my nerves with his constant yodeling. The fall was like waking up; it was time to put an end to these holidays spent together with him. All these years, I felt so uncomfortable in his company, but I acted as if it did not matter. I swallowed so much grief without saying a word.

Paul also decided not to go on holiday with his dad anymore, after spending a terrible two weeks with him in Italy. The old lion could not stop comparing himself to his son, telling him that he was sure he was the one who was the more successful with young women. When Paul made fun of him, the old man replied that he was in fact in love with a woman who aspired to be, one day, the Chancellor of Germany. She was in her thirties and very attractive. Karl told Paul that he was thinking of inviting both Paul and I for a coffee at his place, in order to present us to this woman. Until that point, he had been discreet enough not to talk about his love affairs, but this time I think he talked about the woman just to enrage his son. Paul was indeed very upset, and told him that he should show more respect to me, his mother, and neither he nor I were interested in meeting any of his whores. During these holidays in Italy, my son was calling me everyday, giving me a detailed account of his father's appalling behaviour. I finally had to call Karl to tell him to stay quiet and leave his son in peace. As usual, the old man denied that there was any problem between them. Paul decided to return home earlier than planned, however; he could not stand the presence of his father anymore.

We found out that the Chancellor-to-be was a woman in her late thirties, who was going out with Karl from time to time while having a relationship with another man. She left Karl after having swindled him out of a huge amount of money. He opened a bank account for her in the principality of Lichtenstein.

I served as an alibi for Karl; he told all the women who were going out with him that he was married. They could not ask him too much of the relationship, or urge him to get married. All of them were in their thirties. The 'fresh meat' was regularly provided at my husband's office, mostly young secretaries in search of money. The love affairs did not last very long. The women thought they would be covered with jewels and receive a monthly annuity, but after some time with him, they found out that nothing of the sort ever happened. They soon got bored and left the old man. But he did not have any real feelings for any of them, so the vampire stayed unhurt and was again on the lookout to find another young victim. So many women were eager to have an affair with a rich elderly man.

Paul and I laugh about one woman who showed more tenacity than the others. She was married to one of my husband's employees. She kept bringing him tomatoes, apples and vegetables from her own garden; typical presents coming from a simple woman. My husband lived in a house near a lake, and one day while Paul was sunbathing on the pier, he heard a noise and saw the woman coming out of the water. She had swum from the other side of the lake. Karl was not at all attracted to her. Apparently he told her not to disturb him, but she was stalking him. When she saw Paul she swam back, leaving behind her a bottle floating on the water. Paul fetched it. It contained a message; a poem written on a pink card, decorated with little flowers, all hand made. Paul found it very funny; even his dad had to admit that he was attracting very strange women indeed. I felt for her; I felt for all of them, all these women, one after the other listening to this old devil, believing every word he said, just as I believed him when I first met him.

I often forgot that I was still a married woman. But Karl was there to remind me that he was still in my life. My husband could not accept that I was making plans for the future, and getting on quite well with my life without him being part of it. He tried by all means to control my finances. Money was his only source of power over me. He played with me, refusing to give me any money if he felt I was particularly happy. He took a lot of my energy by keeping me worried until the last moment, before finally sending me the money for which I was asking. But he could not hurt me anymore, and I had no respect for the man at all. I found him small and pathetic, even if he boasted he was one of the best solicitors in the country.

He agreed to go to the island to take care of the sale of the beach property. Afterwards he wanted to invest the money for me and I let him do so, too happy not to have to think about it. I was wrong. After a year, he told me that he made a bad investment, and had lost a huge amount of the money. I suspected he had taken the money for himself. My husband never made bad investments. Why should it happen now? This time I went to see a young solicitor, with whom I had a little fling. He contacted my husband and asked for a detailed account of the investments that supposedly went wrong. Instead, my husband gave him a list of my debts. All those years he had kept account of all the money he had given me; the debts included the flight tickets that he had paid for me and for my son. He even counted every single stay at the Swiss hotels where we spent those horrible holidays with him. I owed him nearly two hundred thousand euros. But instead of being scared, I became very angry indeed and told him that if I allowed him to come to my house it was because he paid for those travels, and those of my son as well. I said that it was not a privilege for us to ski in his company, and I did not intend to pay for any of those holidays. From now on, I would not allow him to put one foot in my house, nor in my garden. I wanted him to disappear from my life forever. Paul called him a thief; for more than a decade he had kept the child allowance in his own pocket, instead of giving it to me for his son. Paul said he would not see him anymore if he did not cancel this ridiculous list of debts immediately. I asked for my money from the property as well. The list of debts was only used as a diversion, to prevent me from asking where my money had gone. But Karl, surprisingly, said that there were things that he would erase from the list of debts, and by a miracle he could recover some of my money.

I really did not care about the money; it was more important to keep a certain standard of living. The solicitor told me that I could not have debts towards my husband because I was still his official wife. He thought that Karl had not divorced me because the marriage status reduced his income tax tremendously. So I made fun of my 'list of debts', and whenever I needed more money I would ask my husband to consider it as one debt more. I did it over and over again. I always attained my goal, even if it was a struggle with this old miscreant.

Chapter 11

After all the trouble in my home country, I did not go back there for eight years. My mother did not talk a lot to me, in fact, she never said anything, just answering my polite questions with 'no' and 'yes'. I was making the conversation, and after some time I did not know what to say to her. She had erased me from her life. Even when I talked about Paul, her grandson, she stayed completely indifferent. My father had mellowed in his old age; he took real joy in talking with me, complaining about my mother's dementia. Too old to drive, he sold his beloved car and travelled by taxi to do his shopping. He took care of the household, giving much importance to his cooking; my mother helped by chopping the vegetables. Sometimes she had her fits of madness and insulted him. My father had a very hard life with her. My brother, the king, came to see them during the weekends. Like he had done for the past thirty years, my father prepared dinner or lunch for his son and his clique. They came, sat and as soon as they finished eating, they left. With our father being old and weak, my brother did not respect him anymore. He seemed to take pleasure in treating him badly. He got into the habit of insulting our father very loudly in front of his friends when the old man dared to defend me whenever my brother dragged my name through the mud.

My last conversation with my father was three weeks before his death. We talked to each other on that day, as if knowing that it would be the last time. I told him everything; the grudge I had for them, for their lack of support and their indifference. He did not know what my brother had done to me. He thought I had sold my property on the island on a whim; my brother told him that I had sold it to be able to throw money around and feed my lovers. When he heard that my brother had abused his power of attorney to steal from me, my father became very sad and was deeply disappointed in his son's behaviour. But I also reproached my father for his silence when my husband left me. He said he thought that Karl was not really going to leave me and that giving no importance to the matter would enable my husband to come back without losing face. I also tried to erase the stigma of the mental disorder that had stuck to me for years, caused by the wicked tongue of my brother and my husband. My father admitted his foolishness to believe them so easily. He thought that I had inherited my mother's insanity. But he realised after some years that I could not be mad after all, because he could see that I was leading a normal life, taking care of the well-being of my son, without the help of a third party. After this open conversation with my father, I felt that, at last, he believed in me and at last, I was relieved of a huge burden. My father had never been perfect but he was a man of integrity and asked me to forgive him for letting me down when I needed him the most.

Surprisingly, on that day, my mother expressed the wish to talk to me as well. She was impatient and frantically urged my father to let her talk to me. She told me with an unusual enthusiasm that my niece was getting married. My brother, wishing to have a great celebration, had already started the preparations. My mother told me to come to the wedding and literally ordered me, at the same time to bring her a nice outfit, shoes, a handbag and a wig! I told her that I could not come because I had not been invited. She told me that I did not need any invitation; I had just to come. All she wanted was for me to buy her a whole outfit for the wedding. She did not care that my brother might throw me out of the party if I came uninvited. But I heard my father rebuking her, that she should stop asking me for expensive gifts.

My cousin Josephine told me that my parents attended the marriage ceremony at church, but my father refused to go to the reception, which took place in one of the most exclusive hotels of the island. As usual, he said that he was sick of all the tam-tam and the showing-off of my brother and his wife. I truly believe that in not going to the reception, my father wanted to demonstrate his support of me, his daughter, who had been totally rejected by my brother and his family.

Some days later, shivering with fever in my bed on a very cold morning, I was woken up by the telephone. I jumped out of bed, thinking it was Paul calling from his boarding school. But I heard the voice of my mother who announced to me without mercy:

"Your father is dead."

But I also heard somebody in the background saying something to her, and I was thought I heard the voice of my own father. Believing wrongly that it was one of my mother's recurrences of madness again I said to her:

"Mother, stop it. I'm as sick as a dog and you dragged me out of my bed to tell me such a silly thing."

She hung up the phone without a word, and to tell you the truth it did not occur to me that I should call her or my dad again. Three days after, I received a call from my cousin Josephine who asked me:

"Do you know that your father has passed away?"

I stayed put, unable to say a word for some seconds, then I told her about the call from my mother and that I had not believed her.

I told her: "Why did you let my mother tell me? She had told me so many unreal things before that I could not possibly take her seriously. Why did you not call me yourself?"

She said: "I did not have the time to call you."

I thought what a hypocrite she was. She always called me for the silliest gossips ever, asking whether I put on weight, and if my husband beat me, but for such a terrible thing as the death of my father, she just did not have the time to give me a call.

My old aunt Juliet wanted to talk to me about my father's death, and it was only then that I started to cry.

My father passed away on a Monday at five o'clock in the morning and they buried him the same day, at four in the afternoon. My brother did everything to stop me from coming to the funeral. Only a few people were there. His old friends and colleagues had not even been informed. He took care of his roses, but he did not have any for his funeral. All the flower shops were closed on that day because it was a bank holiday, and he had only a very few on his coffin. My cousin Josephine reported all this. She was happy to add that my father had not deserved better because he had been such an arrogant man all his life. She even compared his funeral to that of her husband, saying that his had been so glamorous. How ordinary on her part; I wondered how I could belong to this lot. It hurt me to hear her speaking badly about my father, there was no end to it, and even after he had died they could not stop hating him.

But I was appalled that my brother had not even waited for the legal twenty-four hours before burying his own father. All he had in mind was to prevent me from giving my father a last kiss. When people asked where I was, he told them that I could not come because I was ill.

Some days later, a distant relative called to present her condolences and that of her family. She was surprised that I was not at the funeral. I told her that even if I had been properly informed about it, I would not have been able to do the trip in such a short lapse of time and be in time for the funeral. The flight from Munich to the island took twelve or fourteen hours. The woman acknowledged that the funeral had been done in a hurry, and that my brother had been acting strangely that day. He refused to answer their questions about me, saying that it was impossible to talk to me, that I had changed for the worse since my husband had kicked me out of his life. She also asked me why I did not attend my niece's wedding; she knew that I was her godmother. I said that when I separated from my husband, my brother had abused his rights, and I had to take measures to protect my own interests.

I called my mother to tell her how touched I was when this cousin called me because she had thought of me, she had not forgotten that I had bought a small house for her and her family. But my mother shouted at me on the phone:

"How dare that woman call you? Why did she have to interfere?"

The word 'interfere' sounded interesting, it showed me how much my mother was aware of everything my brother was doing to me. She just wanted to isolate me completely from the other members of the family, so that no one would know how nasty my brother was to me. Everybody should only hear my brother's version of the matter. They should assign me all the wrong and think of my brother as a victim.

But my mother would soon be very disappointed by the ungratefulness of her daughter-in-law. Only one year after the death of my father, my mother's life had changed for the worse. My father had been caring for her, day and night. But now she depended completely on my brother, who took her to his house every night.

This displeased my sister-in-law, who did not want to take care of the old woman and showed it without shame. My mother told me how my sister-in-law even refused to talk to her, and how she always came back home from work very late, sometimes at ten o'clock in the evening. She wanted to be sure that she would not be the one having to take care of her mother-in-law. There seemed to be a cold war between my brother and his wife.

One day while I was talking to my mother on the phone, she interrupted me and out of the blue said:

"You…" she never called me by my name, "you do not have a husband. Come back and live with me."

Interesting indeed! When my husband left me, she never told me to come back home. I was not welcome. But now that my father had died, Madam needed a carer, and this had to be me, the worthless daughter. I told her that I could not leave Germany to take care of her because of my son. She answered dryly:

"Your son does not need you. He has his father. That's enough for him."

I felt anger overwhelming me and answered back very brutally:

"And where were you when my husband left me? When I was left alone with my son, struggling; did you comfort me? Did you ever call me once to ask how I was? When my brother emptied my bank account, did you try to stop him? Now you tell me to leave my son to come and take care of you. You tell me that my son does not need his mother, that to have a father is enough for him. How dare you treat us so badly? I am not worth a penny in your eyes, and even my feelings for my son do not count." (I wanted to say my love for my son, but I could not pronounce the word 'love' in front of her.) "You are selfish. I am not your slave. You have always preferred your daughter-in-law to me, being always at her side and covering her with presents and compliments. Just stay with her now."

My mother's authoritative tone and her coldness towards my son and me felt like a slap in the face. When Karl left me, nobody from the family told me to return to the island. They did not want to share the house with us; a house that I had given them. They were ashamed of me, they did not want people to know about my broken marriage. But now, suddenly my mother thought that I could be useful to her. So I should leave my life in Germany behind and sacrifice myself for her. It hurt me even more to see that she did not care about my son at all.

But that was not the end of her meanness; my father's inheritance was obviously my brother's main preoccupation. Some time after this conversation, my mother told me that I had some documents to sign. When I asked her which documents they were, she said that it was all a formality from the bank; she needed to get to my father's account. She needed money. I told her I was surprised to hear that, because she did not have that many expenses, not going out at all and having lost all interest in clothes. She had her own retirement pension and now her widow's. Did she really need more money, and for what purpose? She snapped at me:

"Just sign these documents when I tell you to do so. You do not have to argue. You live far away and you do not know anything about my needs. Your poor brother has all the troubles to deal with, all alone."

The papers arrived shortly afterwards, sent to my husband's office. Karl told me that if I signed them, all the inheritance would pass to my brother's hands.

The documents gave a list of my father's bank accounts. He also had a joint account with my mother for decades. But I could see that this joint account was now under the name of my father and my brother. It was evident that this change of name had been done after my father's death. My dear mother ordered me to leave my son and take care of her as a servant, but she was not willing to give me my share of the inheritance.

I had to sign a letter that my brother had written and it stated that I allowed him and my mother to have access to my father's money. If they thought that they could do whatever they wanted with me, they were wrong.

When I told my cousin Josephine about all this, she acted as if she did not understand a word. She told me that my mother was still my mother, and that she had dementia; I should not be upset with her. But I thought that the love of my mother for her son surprisingly overcame her dementia. She stayed loyal to him and did everything he wanted her to do. My mother's behaviour towards me had nothing to do with her illness. It just showed that she did not feel much for me. I had to admit it and accept it.

I never sent the bank documents back, nor did I sign them. I would wait for the death of my mother to have a share of the inheritance. But I did not know the extent of my brother's tenacity and greediness. He had not said his last word yet.

Chapter 12

After four years Paul went to the United States to study. At university Paul made good friends; very eclectic from their background and culture. He loved his new life. We thought constantly of the future; where would he be after his studies? I have learned to let go, giving my son the full responsibility for his own life. He was now a young adult who knew what he wanted, and I was proud of him. I only hoped that he would not be too far away from me in future.

I had not found anybody with whom to share my life. The men I met were fascinated by my personality at the beginning because I was exotic, in every way. But after some months, the fascination changed to jealousy. They would take off their masks, revealing an inferiority complex. I met the same stereotype of men; birds with broken wings, weak but selfish enough to be looking for any sort of advantage in the relationship. I could feel the anger growing in their little macho brains after spending time with me. They would then try to dominate me. They wanted to mould me, make me become submissive. I should do this and that; whatever they liked in me at the beginning of our relationship, was no longer to their tastes after a while. They criticised me constantly, trying to destroy my self-esteem. I got rid of them without wasting any more time. I started to like my own company, living by myself with my dogs. I was aware that, until now, I had not met anybody with a great personality or who was on the same wavelength. I had let myself be duped by liars, who looked good enough at first. I knew it was time for me to meet someone who would be a real friend first, then a lover. I had to work that out with myself. I was sure I could change, stop attracting the weirdest guys and have at least one normal, reliable one.

Karl was still officially my husband, still using his last weapon, the finances, to keep control over me. I sold the family house to him. I could not stand seeing him coming and going to my house, as if he had all the rights to do so. He was always spying on me. Paul and I looked for another house, far away from Munich. After more than twenty years living in the same town, I'd had enough of running into the same people, calling themselves friends, but who were, in reality, envious of me. When my husband left me with nothing, most of them were eager to know every detail of my private life, telling me how sad they were for me. But when they saw how well I managed to make the best of the situation, they changed towards me, unable to hide their anger towards the 'foreigner'. But what they thought was of no importance at all. I turned my back on them in the hope of a new start somewhere more peaceful. I wanted to be able to relax, live without fear of what my husband might be planning to do me wrong.

One day something most strange happened to me. One morning I woke up and I felt thankfulness. I was sincerely grateful to my husband, to my brother, to my mother, to my sister-in-law and all the others. While being wicked, cruel, selfish and vile, they forced me to search for spirituality, for God's presence, not just as an aloof vision, but real and strong in my everyday struggle to survive. Going beyond the pain of my broken and tired heart, I found freedom, knowing suddenly that everything I had been longing for was in me already. I did not have to search for love anymore, because love was in the very core of me. It was the most extraordinary feeling I have ever had in my life. I thanked all those who, by trying to do me evil, had made me find the good in myself. They played a bad role, and because of them I learned how strong I was.

Paul and I found the most beautiful house, hidden in a village near the Black Forest. I was now far away from city life, and even if sometimes I missed the busyness and the cultural events, I felt better in this luxurious chalet surrounded by pine trees. In the wintertime, the deer came to visit me at dusk, leaving the tracks of their little hoofs in the snow. The birds would come noisily, looking for the food I had left for them. I loved my new home and, while it was in an impeccable state, I decorated it enthusiastically, adding some personal touches to the house, respecting the style of the previous owners because they had very good taste indeed. The house fitted beautifully in its environment. I loved to sit in front of the fireplace with a good book and one of my innumerable cups of coffee, and my dogs taking turns sitting on my lap. It was the life I always dreamt of.

Nobody could understand how I could leave Munich to go and live in the countryside, all by myself. They could not believe that a woman could intentionally choose to live alone. What if something happened to me? But so many things had happened to me already that I was not afraid of anything anymore. I even sent away the housemaid who used to work for the previous owners; she was too nosy and chatty.

I drove to the next town when I longed to be back in civilisation, for some shopping or to go to an art exhibition, however bad the weather might be. I still did my best to look nice and to dress elegantly, and I loved to take some inspiration from the trendy shop windows. I started to socialise, joining an arts and culture club. I found pleasure in sharing my time with intelligent people, and was delighted to receive more and more invitations for concerts and other enriching events. I even opened the doors of my house to some of them, which is something I had not done for decades.

Meanwhile Karl was getting much older. He was losing his power over his solicitors, in the office. They were all getting impatient, expecting him to retire and get out of their way. After all, he was now in his seventies. But Karl clung tightly to his position in the firm. He knew how empty and meaningless his life would be if he stopped working. There were some conflicts between him and some of the lawyers. The atmosphere at work was not good anymore. Karl was losing some of his clients. He earned less money than he used to. He felt that his lawyers were watching everything he did. They were waiting for his next failure that would enable them to give him a golden handshake. But the firm would still keep his name, even after his death. These vultures, who had become rich thanks to my husband's infallible ingenuity, now wanted him to disappear in order for them to take over. What an ungrateful lot! But what a retribution for my husband, he who said openly that for him, his job was more important than his family. I knew how dreadfully hurt he must have been to watch the abasement of his authority in his own office, his master-piece. But he was used to fighting and he stayed put, like an old statue facing the most forceful and violent wind.

Things were not going well for his other family either. His daughter, Elizabeth, made a *mésalliance*. She married a big-boned German man who had nothing but his ego. He refused to follow his father-in-law's advice, and accumulated debt after debt while setting up one business after the other, all of which quickly went into bankruptcy. Ultimately he asked Elizabeth to turn to her father for financial help. At first Karl saved him from his creditors, but after the second time he wanted to be paid back. Poor Elizabeth, who was a hard worker and earned a comfortable salary, had to pay her own father back at a monthly rate. I felt compassion for the young woman; she did not have a good father and chose a man for a husband who was no better. She was scared that her father would disinherit her. Her husband refused to work for anybody, over-estimating his capacities. Every new start in a new enterprise ended up as a catastrophe. But the man was intuitive enough to sense that he was losing his wife. Elizabeth apparently confided in her father that she wanted to end her marriage, even though they had a child together. Surprisingly, she became pregnant soon after, leaving her father baffled by the news. With two small children, the poor woman could not think of a separation anymore.

Fabian, Karl's older son, received an annuity from his father and lived in a little flat near the city of Düsseldorf. He was still unable to work, or drive a car or have a normal life. He now put all his energy in spying on his brother-in-law. He used to stay at his sister's home and he reported everything in detail to his father. He was doing to his brother–in-law what he had done to me fourteen years ago. From what I heard, he also made sure that his father was not too generous to Paul, nor to me. Karl was always complaining how Paul was spending too much money and that he should try to be as economical as his half-brother. He should buy his flight tickets weeks before departure. He should not buy so many clothes. Is he eating too often at restaurants? He was also urging him to finish his studies so he could start working and earn his own money. Paul told him that he did not see why he had to consider his half-brother as someone to look up to, and wanted to spend some more years studying. After all, his father was wealthy enough to pay for his studies.

Chapter 13

One day, by chance, I met some islanders, acquaintances who were in Germany on holiday. After the obligatory small-talk, they told me that the house where my mother lived was now rented to some of their friends. I gave that house to my parents. After breaking up with my husband, my father put the house under my name so that it would come back to me after his death. But with his usual mistrust towards me, he asked that the legal document stipulated the usufruct, which authorized him to use the property until his death.

It was now four years since my father's death, and because of the usufruct, my mother was legally allowed to stay in the house. I wanted her to stay there too. But these people told me that my mother was unable to live by herself now. She was aggressive to all her housemaids and carers, and they all quit after a while. My mother was living at my brother's place permanently, and his housemaid, who had been working for the family for more than thirty years, dedicated herself to my mother all day long.

At that time, I was still calling my mother at my brother's, and she assured me that she was going back to her house a few times a week. Even my cousin Josephine told me that my mother was sleeping in the house from time to time. But these were all lies; my brother was renting the house behind my back, keeping the money for himself. Once more, my mother was his accomplice; legally she could do whatever she wanted with the house, but why keep me uninformed about the rent? I decided not to waste my energy talking endlessly with my brother about it. I would not go back to face the members of my family and plunge back into this dark and sticky marsh. I had struggled for twelve years; I grieved over my broken marriage and accepted the lack of love from my biological family. It was over now. I decided to let go of any feeling of guilt or duty. I was free; at last I found an overwhelming love in myself. I felt happy every day of my life, without reason. I had changed so much, laughing at any foolish thing that anybody would say to me.

I could not do anything as long as my mother was alive. I went to the island a last time, braving my brother who had threatened to kill me if he ever saw me. Karl accompanied me, but I did not want Paul to come with us. It was emotionally very overwhelming for me when I went to kiss my mother at my brother's house. I called the housemaid and bribed her. She told me when my brother and sister-in-law were at work, and I went to their house. My mother was surprised to see me, but she did not show any joy. She was eighty-eight years old, and she was in a dreadful state. Nobody was taking care of her appearance; she who had been such an elegant, beautiful woman. I remembered how my father used to take her to her hairdresser regularly to have her hair dyed black, but now she had white hair hanging like straw at each side of her face. My sister-in-law obviously did not care what the old woman looked like. My mother had been given so many calming pills that she was haggard. But she did look at me intensely from time to time. I washed her feet and gave her a pedicure. She watched me massage her feet, and seemed to enjoy it. But the housemaid started to get nervous, and asked me to leave before my brother or my sister-in-law returned home. I said good-bye to my mother and kissed her, but she did not put her arms around me; she stayed sitting in the straight elegant posture she always took. On the doorstep, I turned to look at her one last time and she suddenly said loudly to me:

"Your brother hates you."

"I know, Mother." I said. I smiled at her and left.

My mother died a few months after our last meeting. Nobody told me. I dreamt of her and of my dad so intensely night after night that I told Karl to call my brother at his office and ask about my mother. Karl was told that my brother was on holiday overseas, and that my mother had died a month earlier. My parents had come to see me after their death, to communicate with me at last. This reconciled me with them, especially with my mother. Sometimes I cry and talk to them; I know that they are around me. At last I have my parents back and I can be their child again.

A lawyer took care of my inheritance and of the sale of the house, but it took me years before I could finally turn the page, leaving the island and its horrible people behind me once and for all. This time, I defiantly insisted that the money would not be invested by my devil of a husband. But I only received some crumbs of what was left after he had deducted the costs of the lawyer. It did not matter; I had showed my brother that I had rights and that he was not my parents' only child.

Chapter 14

Two years later, during the Easter holidays, Paul and I went to Great Britain. After a beautiful drive along the south coast of England, we stopped in front of a nice little hotel, admiring its beautiful, very English garden. Paul was asking me whether I would consider leaving Germany to move to the United Kingdom if he decided to finish his studies there. We were talking excitedly about this possibility when my telephone rang, and Paul and I were brought back to reality. I took the call; something must have happened. I must admit that my first thought was for my dogs, which I had put in a kennel. I always felt bad about leaving them behind. But instead, one of Karl's lawyers was on the phone. I knew that Karl was in Switzerland with his partners. They often had their meetings in Switzerland, where they could ski and discuss internal office affairs, combining pleasure with work. I had talked to Karl the night before, and he told me that they had planned to go skiing early the next day. Something serious must have happened. I had not spoken to any of his lawyers for fifteen years. I heard the man tell me his name; his voice was feverish and he was looking for words. I urged him to speak and finally he said:

"There has been an accident."

I just muttered: "He's dead, isn't he?"

The man stammered dreadfully and managed to say yes. I heard the hypocrite cry, he who, like the lot of them, had always wished for the death of his master. I calmed him down as if what had happened was in no way my concern. I wanted to know how my husband had died and once the man had started to speak, he could not stop. Some Germans have a habit of talking in a very monotonous tone; it is their way of getting in control of their emotions.

Apparently my husband and his colleagues left the hotel at dawn. A mountain guide accompanied them, and they flew by helicopter to the summit of a mountain. The night before, Karl told me how tired he was and I advised him not to overdo it. Of course, he laughed at me, saying that he was a very experienced skier. I think that even feeling unwell; he had no choice but to go with the others. If he had not, it would have been a con-firmation of his weakness. So at seventy-two, he jumped from an helicopter on the summit of a glacier; he was surrounded by vultures, his much younger lawyers, who were all hoping to get rid of him, the sooner the better. The descent seemed more difficult than usual; there was a devilish, icy wind. My husband was soon the last of the group, and the distance between him and the others grew more and more. The slope was too steep to stop at leisure, and when the group reached a platform to catch their breath, they noticed that my husband was missing.

They waited for him, then climbed back and finally called for help. The weather had changed suddenly, and a storm was coming. The guide urged them to descend before putting themselves in danger. Later on, because of the bad weather, even the rescuers had to interrupt the search for my husband. The next day they started to look for him again and, finally, his body was found in a crevasse. The fall had broken his neck, which probably caused an instant death. He was found in a thick block of ice, which the rescuers had to break in order to extricate him. My husband's body was flown to the mortuary in a sack hanging from the helicopter. How strange to know that this cold-hearted man had died in his element: the ice.

I kept calm and asked about the macabre details concerning the expatriation of his body and so on. I insisted that I would organise the funeral. I could concentrate on all the practical sides of the situation, refusing to think about the death of my husband who I had once loved and who, after fourteen years of marriage, had turned into my dreaded opponent; the cause of all my torments.

On the day of the funeral, I wore big dark glasses and an elegant vintage Chanel suit. Paul was very handsome in his dark suit and I was proud of him, looking so dignified in this terrible moment of his life. I held his arm all the time and did not waste one tear; I was not going to make a spectacle of myself. I greeted Elizabeth and Fabian briefly and some of the relatives, whom I knew. I noticed some of Karl's mistresses, who sat at a safe distance from us. Some of them were sobbing loudly.

They were probably crying because they knew that they were not on his will.

I put my wedding ring on the stalk of a rose and threw it into his open grave. After the funeral we left discreetly. We did not want to join them at the '*Leichenschmaus*', a dreadful word meaning literally 'corpse carvery'. Just like in any other part of Europe, it was traditional to offer a meal to those who had come to pay their last respects to the deceased.

I knew that Paul must have felt distressed, but he had lost his dad a long time ago.

I wanted us to say good-bye to Karl in a ritual for the deceased, to help him free himself from the guilt of his being so nasty to us. It was important for me to know that he found peace. So we went to his house near the lake, lit some candles and incense in the living room and prayed. Before leaving, I went into every room to see if the windows were closed. Entering his bedroom, I felt a strong vibration in my head and in my navel, as if suddenly I was suffering from high blood pressure. I knew he was there. I opened his wardrobe and touched his clothes. In a drawer was an envelope on which he had written my name. I put it in my bag without opening it and left the house.

I read the letter much later in the evening; he had written it ten years before.

It said:

Dear Ann,

You have come from your island, so young, with your heart full of love. I have used you as an accessory in my life, a beautiful object for me to show off. You suffered badly when I showed interest in other women, even in your presence.

But I hurt you even more. In our relationship I took the better role, treating you as insipid, criticising you constantly, humiliating you in front of my children.

To make this confession is terribly difficult for me. I sincerely regret all the pain that I have caused you, aware of how impossible it is for me to erase the irreparable.

Karl

I folded the letter and put it back in its aging envelope, on which I wrote:

Dear Karl,

I forgive you. You are a good husband now that you are dead.

Adieu.